CW00340957

Alfie's Quest

Best Wishes

Allan -

First published 2021
Copyright © Allan Giles 2021

The right of Allan Giles to be identified as the author of this work has been asserted in accordance with the Copyright, Designs & Patents Act 1988.

All rights reserved. No part of this book may be reproduced, stored in a retrieval system, or transmitted in any form or by any means, electronic, electrostatic, magnetic tape, mechanical, photocopying, recording or otherwise, without the written permission of the copyright holder.

This is a work of fiction containing references to actual persons and events. Such references reflect the author's present recollections of them over time and may be more fiction than fact.

Published under licence by Brown Dog Books and The Self-Publishing Partnership Ltd, 10b Greenway Farm, Bath Rd, Wick, nr. Bath BS30 5RL

www.selfpublishingpartnership.co.uk

ISBN printed book: 978-1-83952-364-9
ISBN e-book: 978-1-83952-365-6

Cover design by Kevin Rylands
Internal design by Andrew Easton

Printed and bound in the UK
This book is printed on FSC certified paper

MIX
Paper from
responsible sources
FSC® C013604

Alfie's Quest

ALLAN GILES

BROWN
DOG
BOOKS

1962
Chapter 1

After the events of last night, and despite feeling rather sorry for myself, nursing a right shiner of a black eye and a swollen cut lip, I carried out my duties as best I could, all the time saying to myself, I should have done more, got a punch or two in before being put on my arse. It's not just my battle scars that's hurting, but my pride as well; did Moira think I hadn't done enough? I did all I could, given the circumstances. The evening had started off so well, and I was in the throes of having my first full sex lesson, when it all kicked off. The annoying thing is the aggro was nothing to do with me, but when your best mate is involved and girls are screaming their heads off, you have to drop whatever you are doing and get stuck in. Anyway, it's now 7am on this Sunday morning and I have an urgent need to sell myself a packet of aspirin, before it gets busy. The store is open for business, except, considering the time of the year, it's turned out to be a right damp, miserable morning, raining hard, and this inclement weather has steamed up the windows at the front of the store. This helped by the heat given off by the early-morning customers, mostly manual workers returning from the night shifts, some still in their overalls, bleary eyed and smelling rather damp whilst queuing up to buy their morning papers and coughing up their fag orders for the week.

'Morning, Alfie,' said one of the regulars. 'What on earth have you done to yourself? You look as though you have been in the wars.'

'Hello, Jack, yes you could say that. It's a long story. I'm battered and bruised, but I'll get over it. One thing's for certain, I won't forget last night in a hurry.'

'Clubbing it in the city, no doubt?'

'I wasn't actually, Jack, a church dance would you believe.'

'No, I wouldn't believe. Anyway I've got to go; a steak on that eye is what I would recommend.'

It was a busy morning despite the rain, and with just about an hour to go until we close at one – half-day on a Sunday – I wiped the condensation off the inside of the shop window with my coat sleeve and connected to the outside world. Peering out of the window, and this mainly through my good eye as the other one by now was quite swollen, I could see two lads across the road waiting at the bus stop. They were slouched against the wall and looking over at the store.

Initially I paid no attention to them, but after giving another customer his change and kicking one of the paper boys up the arse for being cheeky, I then took another look out the window at these two lads, but more intently this time. Suddenly a real 'oh-shit moment' took place. I recognised one of them being the same fucking idiot that gave me this black eye and mashed lip, and with his mates caused all the trouble at the church dance last night. By their stance they were not waiting for a bus to come along either.

My chest tightened up with an intake of breath and I started to fidget. I could feel a real panic within myself slowly starting to build, at the same time giving me that sickening feeling in my stomach. I called Harry on the store's intercom; he was working in the back warehouse and I asked him to come to the front counter. Well, I say working; he was more likely having his way with Dianne on the potato sacks at the back of the warehouse. A slim girl with long black hair, she could be a bit dim but she was a good worker when not distracted by Harry's advances.

Harry emerged from the warehouse at the back of the store, looking a little dishevelled as he quickly buttoned up his white coat, this being nothing unusual as I have seen it before. He came up to the front counter, also revealing his war wounds from the fight last night, a cut above the eyebrow and bruising around the cheek bones. He was a little older than me, fair haired, normally good looking with the build to match, plus the cheek of Old Nick when it comes to girls.

'You look a lot better than you did last night,' said Harry. 'What did your mom and dad say?'

'Oh, I got a bollocking off Mom for ruining a perfectly good shirt, and Dad's only concern was whether I had given the other bloke a going over too. Sad to say that I didn't, as far as I can remember.'

'You didn't, but Eddie did sort him out.'

'That's good; yes it was quite a night wasn't it? Amazingly I have come off the worst, considering you were the one in the frame, mate.'

'Yes, I'm sorry about that Alf. It was unfortunate but you did save me from further punishment. My face is hurting quite badly as it is. You could have been looking a lot worse Alf, if Eddie had not stepped in when he did. You owe him a drink. It was certainly a good old punch up, wasn't it? Still, it got sorted out in the end.'

'I'm not sure if last night was sorted.'

'What do you mean?'

'Well, tell me if I'm wrong, mate,' I said, 'but I think we still have a problem.'

'Alfie, you've dragged me from something important, what do you mean a problem? And it had better be good, I was just in the middle of something.'

'I bet you were,' I said, as I wiped the window again with my sleeve. 'Take a look out at the two lads across the road.'

We both peered through the window. 'It is them isn't it?' I continued. 'Two of the mongrels who were at the church dance last night.'

Harry decided to open the front door slightly, to get a better look at them.

'Yes, you're right, Alfie boy,' he replied. 'I recognise the one with the flat nose and the looks of a Bull Mastiff, he was definitely there. I might be wrong, but I think, going on the events of last night, he is obviously the ring leader of that gang.'

'Yes, you're probably right.'

Suddenly, as if by magic, we saw these two lads become four and then five, all looking across at the store, mouthing something, probably obscenities, and shaking their fists at the same time. They were gathering mob handed, and no doubt waiting to pounce on us when we left. It's obvious they wanted to finish off what they started last night.

Turning to Harry, I said, 'They are waiting to get us when we leave aren't they?'

'No doubt about it, mate, they're going to give us a hiding. They're annoyed that they weren't able to get the upper hand last night and the bastards have come in numbers to give us a right kicking when we close up.'

'Then as I've said, we have a real problem; I don't think my face can take any more hits.'

'Stop panicking, Alf, we just need to think up a plan and fast, decide what the best thing to do is.'

'A battle plan more likes, five against two are not good odds ... '

* * *

When I think back a week, to last Sunday, what a difference that morning was. That morning started off looking like the beginning of a perfect week. I'd just finished my stint at the grocery store and was looking forward to going on to Lynda's house to have a lark about with my mate Harry, who I had noticed had already sneaked off early through the back gate, avoiding his old man seeing him leave, crafty sod. Harry's dad, Mr Richards, who owns the grocery store, gave me this part time job, just four hours on Sunday mornings to supplement my earnings. I work as a clerk during the week in the city, on the bottom rung of the ladder for pay, being seventeen and with little experience. So working here allows me to put some money aside for holidays and bits and pieces.

Having cashed up, I left the counter tidy for the next day, said goodbye to Mr Richards and made my way over to Lynda's house, which is close by, catching up with Harry. Lynda lives in a council house, nothing wrong with that as we all live in council property round here, except Harry of course – his parents are house owners.

Lynda's house, in fact, is next to the Council Yard, so it's ideal for climbing over the wall to nick materials if we need something. There's always someone who needs a piece of Formica, wood, or a roll of felt, but I draw the line at bricks. Lynda's mom and dad were away for the weekend. I bet Harry was already there spinning a few 45s and jiving with Lynda, feeling her bum no doubt at the same time. Lynda's not his regular girl; we are all just good friends and hang around together, generally having a good time, listening to records and larking about.

When I got there, Lynda's front door was unlocked and I walked straight in. 'Hi guys, how we doing?' I shouted, slamming the door behind me.

I walked down the hall to the sound of drums being played at full pelt. The neighbours wouldn't be happy.

'Alfie listen to this new record,' shouted Harry. 'It's a new release by Sandy Nelson called "Let There Be Drums", what do yer think?'

'Sounds great,' I shouted as I entered the front room. The curtains had been drawn partly across the window. There was a bit in the middle where they didn't quite meet, showing the white net behind. Flames from the early-morning coal fire still flickered and I could see lots of vinyl records strewn on the floor next to the Dansette, music blaring from the turntable. You were somewhat special if you had a Dansette record player, or for that matter even if you had a Goblin vacuum cleaner. Lynda's mom and dad couldn't be short of a bob or two.

Lynda was making drinks in the kitchen, a girl with a great personality, loved life and great fun to be with. She stood out with her bright red hair, well blessed up top and great legs, but she had a fiery temper, to go with the hair, not one to mess with, didn't take prisoners.

Suddenly, as the coal fire flickered into second stage ignition, I noticed a girl loafing in an armchair, looking quite relaxed with her one leg over the arm of the chair.

'This is Moira,' Harry whispered, appearing from nowhere. 'She's a friend of Lynda's and currently unattached, I'll introduce you. Mind you, she's not very talkative, so work your usual magic, show her that crooked smile of yours, and do what you do best, chat her up.

'Moira, this is my best mate, Alfie, not very tall as you can see but he's not bad looking, blue eyes and sports a Tony Curtis hair style. You'll need to watch him though; he's champing at the bit for a steady relationship.' At that, Harry made a quick retreat back in to the kitchen, leaving me like a spare prick at a wedding.

Smiling, I looked across at her, she in turn, with a sultry gaze, smiled back. Dressed in a crisp white blouse, obviously freshly ironed, light blue flared trousers with blue pumps on her feet, she sat up straight on the chair. A good-looking girl with sharp features, pale complexion and long shiny black hair. Her beautiful jade-green eyes followed me as I approached.

'Hi Moira, you're a friend of Lynda's then?' Opening up the conversation.

'That's right, Sherlock. I wouldn't be here otherwise, would I, dummy? We've been friends since our school days.'

'My you've certainly got a sharp tongue,' I said, taken by surprise. 'You want to be careful, you might cut yourself. It's just that I hadn't seen you around here before that's all.'

'Well, we've only recently been seeing each other again. Bumped into one another a couple of weeks ago at the shops and since then been seeing more of each other during the day.'

'Oh right, so in the evening, are you a working girl?'

'What do you mean by that?' she snapped. 'A working girl?'

'Sorry, what I meant to say was, do you have a job?'

'Not at the moment. I'm still looking, like Lynda. What else do you want to know?'

The conversation was hard going but, persevering, I added, 'Well, what do you want to do for a living?' I said, moving towards the kitchen to get a drink.

'Something in the arts,' Moira shouted above the sound coming from the record player.

'The arts, the arts!' I repeated with some emphasis. 'Isn't that sitting in the nude whilst budding male artists with uncomfortable erections pretend not to be interested in your tits?'

'That's typical of you, Alfie,' Lynda said, as I entered the kitchen.

'What's wrong with what I said? That's what happens, isn't it?' I said, as I put my arm round Lynda's waist. She gave me a right old dig in the ribs, saying, 'There's more to art than nudity.' Harry and I returned back into the lounge with the drinks, closely followed by Lynda.

Harry sat on the carpet searching through the records scattered on the rug and put on another 45, titled 'Walking back to Happiness' by Helen Shapiro.

Starting the conversation up again with Moira, I said, 'This singer's from Bethnal Green in London; a year or so younger than me. She has a good voice, don't you think? I've always liked her songs.'

Moira smiled and moved to sit on the sofa nearer the fire. I thought she may have been a little cold, despite the fire still throwing out a little heat, because through her blouse her nipples were sticking out like chapel hat pegs. Now could be the time to see what my chances were at crossing her defences, so I sat down on the sofa beside her and asked if she had a boyfriend.

'Not at the moment' she said with a wry smile. 'But I'm always on the lookout, waiting for the right guy to come along. There's not many about.'

'Shouldn't be a problem for a good looker like you,' I said, shuffling closer, putting my arm round her shoulder as I did so. There was a distinct smell of lavender as I snuggled up real close. We sat chatting for a while, and sensing she was now more relaxed and without any finesse on my part, slowly edged my other hand under the front of her blouse. A voice in my head told me to stop there, but my desire got the better of me. Her skin felt cold and silky smooth, as I slipped my hand further up to find that she was not wearing a brassiere.

'Hey, you're a bloody cheeky one you are,' she said, pushing my hand away immediately. 'Lynda could have warned me about you.'

Not a good start, being so forward and rude; perhaps she wasn't a lie on her back sort of girl, but to my amazement she did nothing. The expected slap in the face didn't arrive. Why was that? I wondered, perhaps she was looking for some boy's company anyway, being braless and all. To my surprise she then dropped her head slowly on to my shoulder. Sighing with relief; I turned my head and kissed her gently on the lips and said sorry.

After a few minutes smooching, I squeezed her hand, gave a wink and backed off, nervous about pushing my luck any further on this first encounter, despite my desire at some point to obtain my non-virginal badge. Anyway, nothing was going to happen, certainly not here in the company of others.

'Alfie,' Harry said, as he finished tiding up the records, 'we need to discuss where we want to go on holiday.'

'That's right, mate, but don't forget you need to ask your old man if we can use the van. Without transport, we're going nowhere. Unless of course you want to go somewhere on the train or in a coach, or charabanc as my old man calls it.'

'Mm, yes you're right; I'll have to ask him tomorrow. The problem is he uses it to go to the wholesalers and for general deliveries. It'll not be easy. He could probably go without it for a week, if he doubles up the orders. I'll speak to him.'

It was a large store that sold most things, except for clothes; it even had a butcher's counter. Harry was a dab hand with a boning knife; he could bone a side of cured bacon in record time, making it ready for slicing, sometimes leaving a little bit too much meat on the bones. These he would slip to me to take home. Mom can knock up a stew from practically anything.

His dad's van is an old bull nose Ford 10 cwt, first registered in 1955. Two tone blue and white, it was green all over at one time until Harry was let loose with a paint brush. It only has windows at the front and big round frog eyed head lamps on the front wings, two doors at the front and two rear opening doors for loading, plus running boards and very little else. It runs well and when Harry and I use it, because it's a two seater, we put a carpet and cushions in the back, which is great for when we have girls on board. Harry fixed a car radio under the dashboard, but because the van's electrics are 6 volt, we connect the radio up to a 12-volt battery in the back. In the evenings we listen to Pete Murray on radio Luxembourg, the station of the stars as they call it, broadcasting on 208, depending on the signal strength that is. We sometimes park up at the local courting spot called the Beacon, a local high point in the area where couples can go and engage in recreational activities or, like us, just listen to the radio, enjoying a better signal. Although you can guess what some recreational activities are with some people, when you see steamed up windows and a bare arse or two.

'I'll see if my dad's in a good mood tonight and ask about the van, and if he agrees,' said Harry, 'you and I can have a chat about holidays next weekend, decide where we want to go.'

'Ok. Perfect, Right girls, shall we put another record on and have a dance?' I said.

Laughing and chatting, we danced and jived the afternoon away to a number of records with Moira and I getting on really well, feeling more relaxed with one another and having the occasional snog. That is until Harry pointed out the time to us, and so we said our goodbyes and both Harry and I left for home, having an early night, preparing for starting another working week in the morning.

Chapter 2

I didn't want to get up on this Monday morning; the bed felt so comfortable and the sound of the rain hitting the bedroom window was not encouraging me at all to go to work. Mom broke the peace, shouting up the stairs for me to get up and ready myself for work. Forcing my eyes open I half looked at the clock on the bedside table, then rolled over, thinking of my time spent with Moira yesterday. What a cracker she is. With my eyes closed I could still see her jade-green eyes giving me the once over and I remembered how silky smooth her skin felt. Was she the one I'd lose my virginity with? I thought she could be. Maybe she was a virgin too, and we could both lose it together?

Mom bellowed up the stairs, 'I'm not going to call you again.'

Realising that I needed to get a move on if I was to catch the 8.15 bus, which arrived in the city just in time to start work at 9 o'clock, I threw back the sheets and made the usual visit to the toilet.

Only had time for a quick bath and to slick back the sides of my hair with Brylcreem. I only do the sides; I like the front on my hair to hang down towards my eyes, giving me the old Teddy boy look, it's still the rage at the moment. I was then down the stairs in a flash, quick bite of toast, a slurp of tea, before grabbing the sandwiches Mom had prepared for my lunch, spam or meat paste no doubt, and then out the door and on my way to the bus stop.

My dad had already left for work; he has worked the last twenty-five years for the same company as a machinist, dirty factory work, something I wouldn't do. He always comes home smelling of suds oil, which for me as a very young kid was, in a way, a welcoming smell – my dad's smell.

I pulled my collar up on leaving the house and ran through the pouring rain trying to dodge the puddles along the way, immediately realising I hadn't cut a piece of cardboard to cover the hole in my left shoe, something I've been having to do until I get some new work shoes. Why is it that it always seems to rain on Mondays and Fridays? When I think of it, I've got years of going back and forth, Monday to Friday to work, earning a living, a depressing thought on a day like today.

The cream and blue bus was already coming down the hill, the number 42, lights on, with its windows steamed up on a day like this, spraying water from side to side as it raced down towards me and looking pretty full with passengers already.

I stuck my arm out and as it pulled up close to the kerb; its tyres splashed water all over the bottoms of my trousers and shoes. Shit, the driver did that on purpose, bastard. The bus hardly came to a standstill as I grabbed the pole at the back of the bus and jumped on to the platform, spinning round in a circle, nearly ending up back out on to the pavement.

'Standing room only,' shouted the conductor.

Pushing inside, I spied an empty seat at the front of the bus and jostled my way through the passengers standing up, the smell of warm damp bodies from wet clothing hit my nostrils.

The bus continued its journey as I elbowed past the last passenger to reach the front seats. As I did so, I banged on the driver's window where he sat cocooned in his cab and called him a shit for getting me wet. He smirks in his rear view mirror at me, so I banged the glass again; sticking two fingers up and mouthing you're a shit head at the same time. Then I tried to sit down on the vacant seat, soon realising why the seat was vacant; a fat woman had placed her equally fat bag on the seat I wanted. She eyeballed me, so I bent forward and eyeballed back, until she moved it, rather reluctantly, onto her lap. I sat down, thinking what do women carry in their bags anyway?

She gave me another look of disdain, as I shuffled to get comfy, that suggested I was a complete pain in the arse, and she wasn't far wrong, considering that barely a cheek and a half was on the seat for the rest of the journey. As the bus sped round corners, I had to steady myself, pressing my hand against the front bulkhead so as not to fall off the seat.

The only time I ever went up top on the bus was night time. If I was with a girl and there weren't many passengers on board, I'd unscrew the overhead light bulb, making it cosy, and you could have a bit of a fumble without anyone seeing what you were up to.

I heard the bus conductor coming to collect the fares, pushing his way past the line of people standing; he must have been upstairs when I got on.

Looking round, I could see the conductor was someone I had encountered on many occasions, a short weasel of a man with shifty eyes, ticket machine over his shoulder and the obligatory corporate conductor's flat cap complete with badge. He had a scar on the side of his cheek, shaped like a tick; it always made me think that someone, at some time, decided to give him a reminder for getting things right in future. He didn't come up for my fare, he would probably catch me when I was about to get off. I'm sure it's a scam on his part, giving me a used ticket someone's dropped on the floor and pocketing the money himself, the ticket punching, scar-faced crook. The bus trundled on, stopping and starting at the various bus stops along the way until arriving in the city centre.

I made my way down Albert Street, still dodging more puddles, to the Electricity Board offices where I work. It's a funny shaped building on the corner of Albert Street and Fazeley Street; wedge shaped with a flat roof, a bit like the Flatiron building in New York – not that I have ever been to New York, just seen it in pictures.

Greeted with the smell of beeswax, used on the desks by the early-morning cleaners, I walked down the corridor, passing the individual offices to get to the general office where I work. Through one of the office windows, as I walked down, I could see Mr Cooper, the office manager, standing up, occasionally looking down at his pocket watch, no doubt checking who's late coming in.

A chubby chap, potbellied, dressed in a smart pin stripped suit, complete with waistcoat, which he keeps his pocket watch in. With his glasses perched on the end of his nose, he glanced at me as I passed his window. He was in overall charge of the general office on the ground floor, including the typing pool and the engineer's office on the second, plus the drawing office on the top floor.

I sat at my desk in the general office, the transport and metering department, and started checking through my usual pile of paper work. It's a large office, lines of desks in sections of responsibilities and importance; a desk close to the window meant you were more senior.

Russell arrived late, which was not surprising as he's late quite often. He sits opposite me and usually comes to work on a motorbike, which on a few occasions he has fallen off. You can always tell when Russell's had a clash with the tarmac; the elbow of his suit coat is in tatters. He's a tall, good-looking chap, a couple of years older than me, jet black hair swept back in to a 'da', duck's arse for short. A great bloke to have a lark around with, always up for a laugh and looks not unlike the rock and roll singer Gene Vincent, who had a big hit with 'Be-Bop-A-Lula', Gene Vincent is a true rock and roller, always wears biker-style leathers, and the last time I saw him live, wore only the one leather glove on the hand he held the mike with. Russell, however, has two gloves but no leathers when riding his Norton Dominator, a 650cc twin-cylinder brute of a machine in black with a bright red petrol tank bearing the scars of many encounters with the road surface.

'Hi Alfie,' Russell said, smiling as he sat down and proceeded to shuffle the papers on his desk, hoping Mr Cooper had not clocked him coming in late via the side door. He whispered, 'Another day another dollar, eh?' followed with a wink.

'Mm, we'd best get to it,' I replied.

Every so often I could hear Mr Thompson, who sat by the window across the aisle from me, give out his usual muffled fart, then look across, smiling accordingly in an apologetic sort of way before looking down at his desk, checking his pens and pencils were neatly lined up ready to do battle on paper. He's getting on a bit and has probably been working here since

Adam was a lad. At least he sits by the window, although I've got used to it now. I think he suffers with piles as well, because he sits on an inflatable ring, and when I first started working here, it cracked me up hearing him trumping away as he sat on his inflatable ring, his nickname of course is Mr Trump.

Then there's Barry Thorn sitting in front of Mr Trump. He's a married man and the talk of the office, apparently, is that he's giving it to one of the girls in the drawing office. I've noticed, he spends an awful lot of time up there.

As the junior clerk in the office, one of my jobs is to take round the morning post and the internal mail. I hate going into the individual offices, because invariably they stop working, hold out their hand for the mail, and without saying a word just stare, suggesting I should have done my rounds much sooner. The exception is the typing pool. I've always got time for them, and they're always pleasant.

Starting my rounds on the ground floor, Mr Cooper was his usual self. He didn't look up or make any comment at all, so I left the mail in the pigeonhole box, just inside his office. I don't think he's forgiven me for sitting in his chair when he was out of the office. One of his fellow managers glared at me through the window one day when passing by, catching me swivelling round and round in it, and reported me.

My next port of call was the typing pool and the engineer's office on the first floor. On entering the typing pool, Miss Marshall was in her office, the proverbial matriarch and office manager, but nice with it. Her office has a large internal window through which she overlooks the typing pool, where lines of girls sit in neat rows facing her, all tapping away on their trusty Imperial typewriters, some faster than others, culminating in the sound of an army of woodpeckers in full swing.

'Come in, Alfie,' Miss Marshall said in her modulated voice.

On entering I handed her the mail, and as usual she asks me what I've been up to over the weekend. She always seems interested and has, over the time I've worked here, given me good advice and support in regard to my social life. A good listener, like an agony aunt you might say, and I feel I can confide in her. Well maybe not everything. Miss Marshall is a very attractive forty-year-old – well I think she's in her forties – smartly dressed this morning, crisp white blouse with frills and black skirt. I have this thing about crisp white blouses.

'Tell me, what you have been up to?' asked Miss Marshall.

'Caught up with my mates, lounged about in the main, met a new girl on Sunday and discussed holidays with Harry, that's about it really.'

'Is she a nice girl, this new girl? Perhaps the one you have been looking for?'

'Yes, she could be.'

'Let's hope so,' she said, taking the post off me.

I could see the girls in the typing pool were having the giggles, so I collected any internal post, thanked Miss Marshall and, red faced, moved swiftly on to the shiny-arsed wonders who work in the engineers' office.

At last I entered the drawing office on the top floor, where everyone sat bent over rows and rows of drawing boards, busy using their T-squares and drawing pens, working on some plan or other. Jane Brown looked round first; you can't help noticing her, good looking, always wearing tight jumpers, with brassieres underneath that give the cone effect, very sexy and she knows it. She smiled at me as I walked past to leave the post in the tray, I'm sure she always knows what I'm thinking when I look at her. The smile followed me as I left and closed the door.

The day progressed and, having monotonously checked loads of invoices for overpayment and highlighting the ones that need attention, I found myself quietly humming 'The Young Ones' by Cliff Richard. Russell flicked a paper clip at me to shut me up. Then the boredom in the general office was soon broken with the sound of rattling tea cups coming from the corridor. Great it was the morning break time.

'Russell, tea time,' I said. 'Time for a slurp and a biscuit.'

The tea ladies, or should I say, the two fat ladies, wheeled in a trolley loaded with teapots, snacks and crockery they had taken off the dumb waiter, which connects all the floors down to the kitchen in the basement. The basement is nothing special, painted brick walls with white tin pendant shaded lights hanging on chains from the ceiling. Apart from the small kitchen, there's a table tennis table where you can play during the lunch hour or sometimes after work if you want to.

The kitchen is home for the two fat ladies and Sid, the janitor. Sid's an old chap, walks with a stoop and a right moaner. He looks after the building and also helps out in the kitchen; he has a go at us young ones every time we go down there. The two ladies lifted up the huge metal tea pots and visited each desk in turn, chipped mugs for the peasants and china cups for the managers. When they reached me and Russell it was a case of, 'Do you want milk, sugar, toast, biscuits, what's it to be, we've got to get a move on,' this spurted out from the fattest one of the two, the other tea lady adding, 'We've had complaints from the top floor that the tea's cold by the time it gets up there.'

How that's our fault I'm not sure.

The morning progresses and Russell asked me to go up on to the roof with him at lunchtime, as he wanted to look over at the office girls in the building opposite, and this because he fancies the blonde one.

'She may not be true blonde, you know; girls dye their hair these days,' I said to Russell.

'Well, it's the blonde one that I fancy, but how we get her attention is the problem.'

'Wouldn't it be easier to wait for her to come out after work? But if you want to, we can eat our lunch up there if you like; I may have an idea as to how you can attract the girl's attention.'

'Stand up there on the parapet with my trousers down?'

'No, you muppet.'

Lunch time came round at last, so Russell and I grabbed our lunch packs, plus the biscuits we had nicked off the ladies' tea trolley. On the way out, we passed the stationary cupboard, so I grabbed a handful of paper clips and a thick elastic band.

We went through the side door to get round the back of the building; it's there where we can jump onto the fire escape that leads up to the roof, and thankfully it had stopped raining. Russell lit up a cig as we clanged our way up the iron stairs of the fire escape. On the way up we have to pass Miss Marshall's office window. I could see she was hanging a picture on her wall. It is a framed black and white picture of someone, whose face looked familiar to me. I stared briefly for a moment through the window, looking at the person's face in the picture. I know I've seen that face before; it's going to bug me now until I remember. Moving on, we continued up the staircase to reach the flat roof, which has a wall round the perimeter but you can still see over and view the city landscape. The air is cleaner at this level, the hum of traffic a mere murmur as it trickled through the streets below. We sat down on a bench and ate our lunch.

'Tell me about your idea then, Alfie?' Russell said. 'How are we going to attract the blonde's attention from up here?'

'I keep telling you, she may not be a blonde,' I said, as I ate my last meat paste sandwich.

'Oh shut up, and don't speak with your mouth full. Tell me what you are going to do.'

'Well, I've got some paper clips at the ready, mate.'

Russell looked a little puzzled. 'What do you mean, Alf, paper clips?'

'I've spent many a lunch hour up here firing paper clips at the pigeons, and I'm not a bad shot; I'll try firing some at the office window where the blond works. The noise could make them look out.'

'That sounds like a stupid idea to me, kid stuff.'

'We shall see.'

We could see the girls in the offices across the road sat at their desks. I lined up the paper clips and bent one in the shape of an S. Putting an elastic band over my thumb and index finger, I hooked a paper clip on the front of the band, drew back and fired.

'I thought you were a good shot. That didn't even reach,' Russell said.

'Give me a chance that was just a practice run.'

I fired the next one and it did ping against the window, but the girls didn't look round.

Using more force on the third attempt, I managed to hit the window loud enough and, eureka, it did the trick, we got their attention. The girls, whose desks were grouped together looked out through the window in our direction.

They saw Russell waving and smiling like the proverbial Cheshire cat, and they in turn gathered round the window and waved back at us.

Russell by now had the girl's full attention and acted out going for a drink, pointing at himself and then the blonde, who was on the far right of the window. The blonde girl, realising it was her he was pointing at, stood to one side away from the rest. With the other girls laughing at his antics, Russell waited for the blonde girl's response. She smiled, then suddenly one of the other girls closed the blinds. Someone of importance must have come into their office.

'See that,' Russell said. 'See that smile blondie gave me. I'm definitely in with a chance with her.'

'That's it, that's it, I remember now,' I said, grabbing Russell's arm. 'It's him.'

'What are you talking about, what's got you all hot and bothered? Remember what?'

'The person in the picture in Miss Marshall's office, I'm sure it's that Australian singer Frank Ifield, a good-looking bloke, just released a new single called "I Remember You". You must have heard the song? It's a great song; I can only imagine Frank Ifield is a favourite singer of hers, or she knows him personally. Anyway you've definitely got the hots for blondie girl, and knowing you, yes, you could be in with a chance. Shit, look at the time, we'd better make our way back down and get back to work or Mr Cooper will be on the warpath.'

The afternoon dragged on with some people working, others trying to look busy. Mr Thompson continued to trump away, glancing up with his usual smile. Bill Jones, who sits behind him, buried his head in his papers, another old chap, looking as if he came with the original décor.

The silence by mid-afternoon was broken with the sound yet again of the two fat ladies bringing the tea trolley into the office, but this time leaving it just inside the general office for the staff to help themselves, this being normal practice in the afternoon as they finish earlier than us, leaving it to Sid in the basement and others to sort it out afterwards. Usually, after tea break, it's left to me and Russell to collect up the cups on each floor and load them onto the dumb waiter, lowering it all down to Sid in the basement.

With the afternoon break over, I left Russell collecting cups on our floor and went upstairs to do the same, starting on the top floor. Having given Jane another look over, I gathered up all the cups and tea pots and loaded the dumbwaiter, lowering it down to the second floor. You know when it's reached the right floor by the set markings on the pulley rope, so with the correct markings in place I ran down to start collecting in the typing pool.

After running downstairs I straightened my tie and entered the typing pool. I acknowledge Miss Marshall through her open door and carried on, gathering up the cups from the typists who were tapping away on their Imperials, not looking at the keys, just reading from notes. Some of the girls looked up as I walked round and started to giggle; they've caught me ogling their tits. Red faced again, I left smiling and with a bit of a swagger. I lightly knocked on Miss Marshall's open door and entered.

'Hello,' we both say together.

Miss Marshall asks, 'Are you feeling a little better now you've met someone else?'

She knew about a relationship I'd had with a girl previously, a girl I was truly in love with but which didn't last, and ended with the girl going off with an older man. He probably had more experience in the sex line, unlike me. It cracked me up for a couple of weeks or more; she was the first real girlfriend I'd had, first love and all that. But I kept thinking that maybe it was because he had a car, rather than for his sexual prowess. Anyway, I eventually got over it, and in part thanks to the support from Miss Marshall.

'Yes, I feel good thanks,' I replied. 'As I mentioned this morning, I've met this new girl Sunday afternoon. Her name's Moira, we will have to see how it goes. Miss Marshall, I can't help noticing the man in this picture on your wall, he reminds me of the singer Frank Ifield. Looks so much like him.'

'That's because it is him, very handsome man don't you think? And I've been a fan of his for some time. I like his music, he has a powerful voice and it's different from the norm,' she said.

With that, I reached over to pick up Miss Marshalls cup and could have drowned in the lovely perfume she was wearing and would have loved to have had her hold me close to her chest.

Gathering up the rest of the cups I left to load them on to the dumbwaiter in the corridor outside, Russell would be waiting to load up all he had collected downstairs. So I placed everything in and started to lower it down gently, otherwise it's off at full speed like a dog out of the traps.

When I got downstairs, Russell had pushed the loaded tea trolley into the corridor and started to load the crockery onto the dumbwaiter, piling it up, emptying the trolley as fast as he could.

'By the way, I told you it was Frank Ifield in the picture.' I started to sing Franks latest song – 'I remember you'.

'You're still going on about that?'

'Yes, Miss Marshall, confirmed who it was when I picked her cup up. The guy in the picture is Frank Ifield.'

'Whatever, mate,' said Russell, putting the last cup on.

'Hang on a minute, don't you think you should take some of these crocks off? It looks overloaded to me. We can't send it down to Sid like that, it needs two loads.'

Russell laughed, 'Screw it, just lower it down.'

'I'm telling you, mate, it's overloaded.'

'Stop worrying; I'll pull the peg out, you just lower it down, its ok.'

Reluctantly I held on to the rope and Russell removed the brake peg holding the lift in place. It dropped slowly at first then picked up momentum because of the weight. I tried to hold on to it, but the pulley rope started to burn my hands as it gathered more speed and I had to let it go, a draught of air rushed up the shaft and we heard an almighty crash as it hit the buffers in the basement, spewing out its contents.

Sid's voice echoed up the shaft. 'You bloody idiots, I know who you are. You did it on purpose, and I'll have you pair before the days out.'

At this Mr Cooper's office door started to open, I looked at Russell and he looked at me, us both making a quick exit into the general office, grinning self-consciously at one another. I murmured, 'I bet Coopers wondering what all the commotion's about.'

Settling down at our desks, the afternoon soon went by with everyone trying to finish off their work. Clocking off time couldn't come soon enough. With minutes to go before leaving, Mr Thompson started shuffling his papers and making sure his pens and pencils were in line and in the right order for the next day. He then stood up and, having lifted up his inflatable ring, he blew into it, just in case it had suffered a loss of pressure over the day. When his cheeks turn red you know it's full, he then carefully placed it back on his chair ready for the next trump to take place.

'What's your next move with the blonde then?' I asked Russell, straightening my desk and making sure I had left nothing unfinished before leaving.

'I'm going to do what you suggested and wait outside her office building for when she comes out, then ask her if she fancies having a drink with me or a night at the flicks. The bike and my good looks should be enough to impress her.'

'Modest or what? You cocky sod and I suppose it will be in the one-and-nines at the pictures?'

'No, the two bob seats at the back.'

Well I'm straight off home. I need to catch up with my mate, Harry, we're deciding where to go for our holidays and whether or not to go to the church club dance this Saturday night, so I'll leave you to it, mate, and wish you luck.'

The bell rang out whilst I was speaking, bang on the stroke of five o'clock; time to go home. Chairs shuffled throughout the building, followed by loud footsteps as people charged down the wooden stairs, and with a mass exodus we all started making our way to the front door after another day at the office. Fellow workers were chatting about their day as we made our way down the corridor, slagging off their manager as usual. I caught sight of Sid the janitor waiting near the exit door, scanning the scene, and he wasn't there for the pleasantries. Wishing Russell and I goodnight was not on his agenda, so turning our collars up and ducking low we managed to sneak past him and slip out unnoticed.

As I began my way up to the bus stop I heard Russell's motorbike growling, I turned round to see him sitting astride his bike outside the offices where the blonde girl works, hopefully impressing her with his 'Norton Dominator' throbbing away. I will say this about Russell, he's a persistent bugger I'll give him that. If he wants something, he'll push it to the limit and only back off when he hits a brick wall. No doubt I'll hear all about it tomorrow.

The rest of the week was pretty much uneventful, Russell did get his date with the blonde, lucky sod. They were off to the pictures Friday night, and I asked him if he was planning on sitting in the back row.

'There's no need for that, Alfie,' he smirked. 'We're only at that friendly get-to-know stage.'

Chapter 3

Saturday's my lie-in day. I looked forward to it all week, not having to get up for anything or anyone, except to think about Moira. I've had her in my thoughts all of the time.

Dad's shelled out and had a telephone installed. It's a big thing round here, having a telephone, a bonus not having to go down to the telephone box on the corner anymore. It's never clean, stinks of pee, you need to be an arm wrestler to open the door and you're lucky if it's working; generally you find someone has pulled the cord from the handset or smashed the cash box open. I'm going to try out our new telephone this morning, giving Harry a ring and seeing what he's up to this evening.

Having eventually got up, Mom shoved a cup of tea in my hand as I walked into the front room to use the phone.

'You're late getting up, son, so it's just some toast for you,' said Mom.

'Yeah that's ok, but can you chuck an egg on it?'

Having picked up the receiver, Dad clocks what I'm doing as he walks past the door and shouts, 'Don't stay on there too long, I'm not paying out three pounds a quarter for a telephone so you can talk to your mates all day. In fact you can give your mother some extra board money, help pay for it. An increase is long overdue. You get off lightly with your mother, she's far too soft on you.'

I can't pay more money out, I thought, not with holidays on the agenda.

Ignoring Dad, I continued and dialled Harry's number. It rang out for a while before Mr Richards answered.

'Can I speak to Harry please, it's Alfie.'

'That depends if he has customers, they always come first.'

Harry's dad is ok, always on the case, looking for the next shilling, if you know what I mean.

Harry came on the phone, asking me if I had only just got up.

'Yeah actually, I have, but it is Saturday. I only wanted to know if you've had any more thoughts on where to go on holiday, and to ask if you're still going to the church hall dance tonight? I think Lynda's going and Moira, it could be fun. There's a live group playing and they're just starting out, so need some support.'

Harry said he was up for the dance but with regard to holidays hadn't given it any more thought, except to say his dad wasn't in the best of moods so he hadn't got round to asking him if we could borrow the van. He then said his dad was shouting that customers needed serving.

'Look I have to go, let's talk about it at the dance tonight, I will see you there at about seven pm, and we can have a good chat about holidays then.'

'Ok, that's great, I'll see you there, and I've spoken with Mom and asked her if she can come up with any ideas where we can go on holiday. She did say she'd look at some places for us to consider, so see you later.'

I spent the rest of the day helping around the house, keeping busy in the hope no more would be said about me contributing more money towards the housekeeping.

Alfie, how do fancy going to Blackpool?' said Mom. 'There's always lots to do there, or Margate, that's where your dad and I will be going. You could always come with us.'

Dad likes Margate, a resort where we've been often as a family, always staying in the same bed and breakfast place, Dad splashing out sometimes for evening dinner as an extra.

There's an entertainment complex called Dreamland, a theatre-type club where they have various artists on. Mom and Dad partake in games and Dad would get up to sing a song or two. Dad's voice isn't bad; he always gets a round of applause for his rendition of 'Some Enchanted Evening'. Dad told me the song was originally recorded in 1949 by Ezio Pinza, although, he reckons he sings it better. But then he would, wouldn't he.

'Sorry Mom, Margate's out for me, I've been there too many times already. Harry won't want to go there either, it's not his sort of thing. Maybe you can think of somewhere else, somewhere we've not been to before perhaps.'

After tea, I went upstairs to get ready for the dance tonight. I had a bath and decided to wear my collarless single-buttoned jacket I recently bought. The navy blue over a clean white shirt, together with my best slacks, will look great. I also decided to wear my black chisel-toed shoes I got for Christmas. I'm determined to look my best tonight and hopefully impress the girls, especially Moira.

Having got all togged up, I slapped on some Aqua Velva aftershave. There was a definite need to smell nice; I just might get to dance real close with Moira. I checked my hair in the mirror, smoothing the sides down with my hands, and flicked my quiff into shape with a shake of the head, thinking it's as good as it gets.

All set, I shouted bye to Mom and Dad; adding that I wouldn't be back too late, and headed off for the church round the corner. I was a nice evening, calm and quite warm, not raining for a change, so no need for a top coat.

Ten minutes later I approached the church rooms and saw lots of people going in but no Moira. I would be well pissed off if she didn't come. I joined the queue to go in, keeping my back straight and feeling pretty good in my outfit. Having paid the two shilling entrance fee, a charge that goes towards the upkeep of the church rooms – the band plays for free, they're just happy to practice together and gain more experience – I walked into the hall and could see a good crowd had turned out to support the dance and the band, including Lynda, but Moira was nowhere to be seen.

Mr Ellison, the church warden, I noticed was also here, he would pop in and out during the evening, checking everything's ok and there's no riff raff in causing trouble. Alcohol is not allowed, hence everyone keeps any drinks they may have well-hidden, and to date he's certainly not caught anyone drinking, and all the dances so far have gone off without incidents.

Harry and I love to dance, not together of course, although these days you can just get on the dance floor and join in. Then there's Eddie, another friend of ours, now he's a great dancer and he'll try to commandeer the girls all night, not giving many of us lads a look in. He is a nice bloke though; a stand-out handsome sort of guy, always wears Cuban heel shoes, which make him look taller, always a flashy dresser. His pencil moustache, slick-back hair style and his Latin looks draw the girls like a magnet. You can always tell when he's on the dance floor; he stamps his Cuban heels to the beat of the music, and can jive or rock and roll better than most. However, if you saw him when he's working he doesn't look quite the part then, he works as a milkman at the local Co-op dairy, throwing crates around, delivering bottles of milk.

The hall is a good size with a sprung wooden floor, which is great for dancing, the open timbered roof seems to work for a good sound and there's a stage at one end where tonight's band would be playing. Tables and chairs sit around the walls leaving plenty of room for dancing.

Mingling with the crowd I looked for Harry, but couldn't see him. Boys were in groups eyeing up the talent and the girls were doing what girls do best, chatting and giggling amongst themselves. I spied Lynda chatting with some other girls but still couldn't see Moira.

'Hi, Lynda, good to see you, has Moira decided not to come then?'

'Hello, Alfie, it's good to see you too. She said she'd come if she could. It'll depend on her dad; he's a bit strict and does keep tabs on her.'

The band were tuning up on stage, checking their equipment, four of them, two on guitars, one on drums and a singer. Well I think he's the singer, looking pretty with his shirt collar turned up, trying to look cool and sexy.

The band kicked off with a Chuck Berry number called 'Come On', which he released last year, and although the music sounded a little like it should, the guitar playing sounded a bit ropey at times. But, considering it was their first performance, there were bound to be a few hiccups. The singer, who didn't sound too bad, was curling his lip up like Cliff Richard does, or the king himself, Elvis Presley.

Eddie was already on the dance floor eying up his options as to who to dance with next, his heels tapping away as if on tick over.

Moira at last entered the hall, looking really sexy in a bright red blouse, short black skirt and white knee-length boots. A black beret perched on the side of her head finished off her outfit. She was closely followed by Harry and both spotted me and pushed their way through the crowded danced floor.

Harry strutted over with his usual swagger, and looking good in a new blue shirt with matching tie and his blond hair all greased up for the occasion.

'Hi mate, been here long?' Harry asked.

'Not long, the group is just warming up and they don't sound too bad for their first gig here.'

'What name do they go under?'

'Haven't a clue. I'll have to ask Eddie what they call themselves, he'll know.'

I was a bit nervous now Moira had arrived, seeing her all dressed up, looking very sexy and so much older. 'Hi Moira, you look stunning. It's so nice to see you, I thought for a minute that you may not come.'

'Mom was ok about me coming, but Dad, he's always protective of me, but Mom talked him round by suggesting he should give me a lift here and pick me up from Lynda's after the dance. Anyway you look very smart yourself tonight, Alfie. Like the coat.'

'Thanks,' I said, lightly touching her arm and whispering, 'please save the last dance for me.'

'Harry, you talk to Lynda and Moira, I'll go and ask Eddie what this group call themselves, that's if they even have a name.'

Eddie, meanwhile, was giving it large by himself on the dance floor, stamping the wooden floor with his Cuban heels; everyone giving him room, watching his moves.

'Hi Eddie, what do you think of the group?'

Eddie stopped thumping the floor for a moment, 'I think they're pretty good, considering they haven't been together long, as a band.'

'What's the group's name?'

Eddie laughed. 'I don't think they've come up with a name yet, how about the "The Four Dicks"?'

Two girls dancing a jive close by heard him and both started to giggle; Eddie reached out, grabbing the hand of one of them, spinning her round and leaving me to dance with the other one. Typical of Eddie, leaving me the worst looker, pig tails, glasses with thick lenses, danced like a robot and looked as if she was in a world of her own.

I could see Harry laughing his head off and Moira in the background, trying not to look at all interested in me dancing with someone.

'You watch,' said Harry to Lynda, 'when this dance finishes, Alfie will come over complaining about Eddie stitching him up. But he likes it really, gives him a chance to try to copy Eddie's style of dancing, without success I might add.'

At that the group kicked in with another rock and roll number, and Moira moments later was suddenly on the dance floor. She grabbed my hand, wanting to dance with me, leaving robot girl to simply walk away.

'That was a bit rude of you,' I said.

'Well, do you want to dance with me, or Miss Pig Tails?' said Moira.

I smiled, saying, 'You of course.'

The hall by now had filled up nicely, and having danced to a couple of numbers, Moira and I left the dance floor, returning hand in hand to the others.

'Alfie,' said Lynda, 'those fellas sitting over there in the corner, they keep looking across at us; I've not seen them in here before, have you?'

'No, not in here,' I replied as I glanced across at them. 'They look the sort that shouldn't be in here, especially the one in the middle with the squashed nose and eyes close together; he's an ugly bastard if ever there was one, probably comes from a long line of ugly bastards. I'm not sure, but I may have seen him somewhere before but can't remember. Anyway, not to worry, Mr Ellison will hopefully have clocked them before leaving. He'll be back later to have another look round.'

The band kicked off with another number, with Moira asking, 'Are we going to have another dance or what?'

'Yes,' I replied. 'I thought you would never ask.'

'The Four Dicks' were playing a number called 'Peggy Sue'.

I love dancing to this song by Buddy Holly, another hit song of his is called 'That'll Be the Day', another good one to jive to.

The singer in the group was doing his best to sound like Buddy, but didn't come close, however, it was nice dancing with Moira. We had a couple more dances, during which time the ugly bastard in the corner was still giving us the evil eye. I pointed this out to Moira, asking her if she had noticed and if she know any of them. Moira shook her head, but agreed they looked trouble, and with the song having finished we went and sat back down.

Mr Ellison, the church warden, suddenly appeared in the

hall and took a cursory look round at everyone, no doubt making sure the band were not too loud and, having done his rounds, smiled and left, probably not coming back to lock up until 10pm when it finished.

Moira said she was going to the toilet and, as is the norm, when one girl goes the other goes too and so Lynda trotted off behind her.

At this point Eddie came over and sat down, saying, 'Those guys over in the corner are from the Barr council estate, Alf, a rough lot. Keep well away, we don't want to be mixing it with them.'

'I don't want to be mixing it with anyone, but they do look a mean bunch.'

'Don't worry, they're probably all wind and piss.'

'That's it,' I replied, 'that's where I have seen the ugly one before. I went to a dance once at a community hall over their way and he, the ugly one, the one with a face like a Bull Mastiff, he was making trouble then with someone. They've come here for one reason or another though and it's not dancing. What do you say, Harry?'

'Not sure. mate but I may have the answer,' replied Harry, all eyes were now suddenly focused on Harry.

'Come on then, tell us more,' said Eddie.

'I'm pretty sure the Bull Mastiff was in the store a week or so ago. Dad caught him shoplifting and threw him out.'

'Let's hope you've got that wrong, mate' I said, getting up. 'I've come here for a good night out, not a punch up.'

At this point I decided to go to the toilet myself, not that I needed to, but just to meet up with Moira for a quiet moment.

As I approached the men's toilet, Moira was just coming

out of the ladies' and stopped in front of me.

'You going for a pee too?' she asked.

'No, just stretching my legs and to steal a kiss from you, after which I'll see you back in there.'

I put my arms around her, pulling her close, and we kissed, her lavender scent filled my nostrils. She then took my hand and pulled me over to the other side of the corridor, backing straight into the cloakroom, dragging me in with her.

It was a dimly lit room, with only two small church-like leaded windows, rows of wooden benches with coat pegs above that had cassocks and surplices hanging from them. Despite the fusty smell of the place, we immediately embraced again and she pulled me to the back of the room, pushing me up against the wall where no one could see us if they came in. We carried on kissing, I slipped my hand inside her blouse and fondled her firm breasts, her nipples were so proud and I just hoped that my hands were not too cold.

It became clear to me that, maybe, just maybe, Moira was not a virgin after all, despite her dad being strict with her. Could be why she was up for it, perhaps she had rebelled in the past. Was this the moment where I was going to lose my virginity and leave the fantasy world of sex? And all this in the house of the Lord. I hoped I had his blessing.

Moira, kissing me even harder, responded by opening my fly and found that my penis was standing up prouder than a bantam cock. She lay down on a bench, straggled her legs either side, looked up at me and smiled, slowly resting her head down as she lay back. Her black beret fell to the floor as she pulled up her skirt and lifted her lily white knickers to one side. This surely had to be that moment, and although totally unprepared as I was for this, I would have to throw caution to the wind. With my heart now beating like a big bass drum, my trousers having slipped right down, my cock having sprung up to attention and throbbing like a septic toe, I was about to penetrate the unknown and sing 'Hallelujah' at last.

Suddenly the door to the cloak room burst wide open with a loud bang, as it hit the wall behind. Who the fuck is that? I thought, jumping up and peering over the cloaks, still with my trousers round my ankles and Moira holding on to my legs. It was Lynda silhouetted in the doorway, in a flood of tears and obviously very upset, as she shouted out, 'Alfie, come quick, we need you.'

Wrong choice of words, I thought, as I pulled up my trousers at breakneck speed. Moira just gave out a sigh as she rolled her eyes back, before she, too, raised herself up to see what all the commotion was about.

'There's a fight, Harry has been set upon by a couple of those chaps from the Barr Estate. Hurry Alfie, it's all kicking off in there.'

Moira, with her mouth wide open and in state of limbo, sat back down as I quickly did up my fly and ran out of the room, overtaking Lynda in the corridor and on into the hall to find Harry on the edge of the dance floor defending himself against two lads who were raining blows down on him. The girls were crying and screaming, the band was playing more out of tune than normal. I could see that the ugly one, armed with something, was about to wade in as well. I charged forward, pushing him out of the way, stepping in between Harry and the two lads who were attacking him, hoping to break things up.

Trying to hold his ground, Harry said, 'Glad you could

make it, where the fuck have you been?'

The next thing I knew was being hit across the face with something, hit like I had never been hit before. My eyes spun round like the rollers on a fruit machine, leaving me staggering all over the place.

Eddie, who had entered the fray, his eyes like organ stops, charged into the ugly one who'd done the damage with such a force; hitting him square on the chin, sending him reeling back over a table with drinks going everywhere before smashing into the chairs behind.

At that, and still reeling from the assault on me, I stumbled backwards, feeling a pain enveloping my face, and dropped to the floor like a sack of potatoes. I must have blacked out for a time during the rest of the mayhem.

Harry and Eddie by now were being helped by others in the hall, preventing any further attacks from these Barr Estate scumbags.

Moira and Lynda were fussing over me when I started to come round and I could hear Mr Ellison's voice, who had now arrived, shouting, 'Now lads we'll have none of this,' in his church-like manner, quickly moving everyone aside and, upon realising the situation, he evicted the Barr Estate lads and restored order. He then asked the band to play their last number whilst the rest of us straightened up the hall and got things back to normal.

As we started to leave the hall, Mr Ellison said to us, 'Tonight's episode is not acceptable, and when the vicar hears about it, there may not be another church dance held here in the future.'

Meanwhile, I was more concerned about how my face was

looking and the state of my clothes. As I looked down, my white shirt had blood all down the front and was now looking like a Red Cross flag. Apparently I was hit by the ugly one with some sort of studded belt. No wonder I was in such pain, but then Eddie did sort him out. After we gathered ourselves together, we all left the hall together working on there being safety in numbers, and went to Lynda's house to get cleaned up and attend to our cuts and bruises.

'You couldn't have gone home like this,' said Lynda, as she applied an ice pack on my eye, 'your mom would have a dicky fit. Now you hold this pack on whilst I take a look at Harry.'

Moira proceeded to wipe the blood off my face; her soft touch soothed me with every gentle wipe she made, easing the pain that I was feeling at that moment.

'I don't think a plaster on my top lip is going to work,' I said, as I looked into her beautiful eyes. Moira applied it anyway.

By now we had all calmed down a little and with the girls' help got ourselves cleaned up somewhat. We all kept quiet when Moira's dad came for her, Harry and I kept well out of sight and then, after a cup of sweet tea, we also decided to make our way home.

Chapter 4

I pulled the latch key out of the letter box and crept in, so as not to wake anyone up. Having got undressed, I went for a piss and crashed out on the bed, with all and sundry going through my brain box until eventually all thoughts faded and I dropped off to sleep.

Having recovered somewhat from the night before, I got up with my face aching and a raging headache. I took a look in the mirror at my rather bruised and battered face, not a good look that's for sure.

Washed and dressed, I put a fresh plaster on my cut lip and went down stairs to show my bruises and face the music. I explained what had taken place, but I think Mom was more concerned about my shirt.

'I will never get this shirt clean,' she said, 'and just look at your face.'

Dad just said, 'I hope you gave as good as you got,' adding, 'I thought they were all church goers that went to the dance. Some church goers!'

I got on with buttering my toast, choosing to ignore him.

'Who started it anyway?' Dad said.

Slapping my knife down, I said, 'The ones that caused all the trouble were not from round here, Dad, in fact, in a way you can blame Harry's dad, because apparently he caught one of the trouble makers shoplifting a couple of weeks back and kicked his arse out the door. I expect he found out somehow that Harry would be at the dance and decided to take his revenge, bring a few of his mates along and lay into us. Anyway, Dad, I have to go or I will be late for work at the store.'

'You can't go to work like that.'

'No choice, Dad, there's only Harry and his dad working this morning.'

Despite the rain I wanted to get to the store a bit early and find out how Harry was, and if he looked any worse than me, he too probably got it in the neck as well from his old man …

* * *

So here we are, back to this Sunday morning at the store with Harry and me, still trying to think of a plan, a battle plan, to get us out of the situation we find ourselves in. Every time I peer out of the window I'm frightened that there will be another mongrel joining the pack to knock seven bells out of us when we leave.

The front door opens. Mr Richards, Harry's dad, comes in, having been out in the van delivering papers that the lazy paper boys had missed on their deliveries.

'Morning, Mr Richards,' I said.

'Good morning, Alfie,' he replied, 'but it wasn't a good night at the dance was it, by the sound of it, and by the look of your face.'

'No it wasn't, Mr Richards. Harry's obviously told you what happened.'

Not knowing what Harry had said to his dad about last night, I quickly walked past and got on with tiding up the counter.

As soon as Harry's dad had disappeared into the back warehouse, I asked Harry what the plan of attack was going to be. Run as fast as we can when we leave or stand our ground and face the music, even though five against two are not good odds.

'I'm not one for running,' Harry replied, 'except from the law.'

'Speak to your dad and ask him what he thinks we should do, he might get the van out and give us a lift.'

'He'll be cashing up and wanting his Sunday lunch, but I'll ask.'

Harry told his dad about the gang over the road and that they were out for revenge for last night, but he was not prepared to get the van out again. He did say, however, that he would call the police if there was going to be any trouble as he was concerned they might smash one of the shop windows; they were plate glass and would be costly to replace.

What about us two? I'm thinking. Don't give us a thought.

Harry, however, said he had an idea and picked up the phone, quickly dialling out.

'Who are you calling?' I asked.

Covering up the mouth piece he replied, 'Eddie at the dairy.'

By now Harry was through to the dairy. 'Hello is it possible to speak to Eddie Morgan please?' I just listened in.

'Oh, tell him it's Harry.'

You could hear whoever he was connected to calling Eddie's name. The voice echoed through the speaker system inside the vast building of the dairy, which at that time of day is normally full of empty bottles, crates and milk floats, everyone having finished their milk rounds.

In a moment or two Eddie had walked into the cash office with his takings, asking who it was on the phone. Harry's name was mentioned.

'What the fuck do you want? I'm in the cash office trying to pay in and clear off.'

Harry explained the situation we were in, and could he possibly help in some way, seeing as how he was involved in the action last night, or if he had any thoughts as to what we could do other than run the gauntlet.

'Who am I, the all seeing eye or something?' Eddie replied. 'What do you expect me to do?'

'I don't really know, but we are in a bit of a fix here to say the least, mate.'

There was a pause in the conversation for a moment, before Eddie said, 'Look, we are just finishing up here; once that's done I will be with you in about twenty minutes or so.'

Harry put the receiver down and started to explain.

'I heard what he said to you, I don't think he's too pleased about it though.'

'He'll be ok; anyway, it's more reassuring with three against five, better odds.'

Harry and I kept on peering through the window hoping that no more lads had joined the wolf pack.

The minutes slowly ticked by, and with the last customer having left the store, Mr Richards started to jangle his keys to lock up. We dragged out the time putting things away, as slowly as we could, hoping Eddie would not be delayed.

'It may be just all show on their part and will come to nothing,' said Mr Richards, jangling his bunch of keys yet again. 'The weather has cleared up now as well, so you two leave. I will keep an eye on things and, as I've said, if they look as though they are going to try to mix it with you I will call the police.'

Harry and I went out the back door, but we still had to pass by the front of the store. Having walked round the front with our collars up, we stepped up the pace and, sure enough, as I looked round, the dog pack started to follow us on the other side of the road, shouting abuse. Both Harry and I said in unison, this is it; we are in for a good hiding. Our pace quickened, stretching our strides a bit more, hoping it didn't look as though we were on the run, but we sure as hell were.

They in turn stepped up the pace and started to cross the road towards us. Their footsteps could be heard getting louder and within seconds the ugly bastard, with his mates, was right on our backs.

With no time to run further, Harry and I turned both in tandem to face the music, clenching our fists, ready to defend ourselves as best we could against five; the odds were certainly not on our side. The cheeks of my arse started to twitch and tighten up and my right leg started to shake uncontrollably with the thought of us being on the verge of an imminent bashing, no doubt sustaining more cuts and bruising. I moved shoulder to shoulder with Harry, both backing up to the privet hedge bordering someone's garden and stood our ground, waiting for the dog pack to pounce.

Then without warning, the sound of an electric motor whirring and screeching at full belt could be heard, together with the squealing of tyres, closely followed with the clatter of empty milk bottles dancing up in their crates. These sounds got louder and louder and the dog pack, who were about to set about us, stopped in their tracks. Suddenly, just like when you watch a cowboy film and the cavalry charges in to rescue the settlers in the wagon train, around the corner came a Co-op milk float virtually on two wheels, headlights on, horn blowing and fully loaded with Eddie and his milkmen friends from the dairy. Three in the front, with three hanging on the back, all still dressed in their white coats, shouting loudly as they approached us and the dog pack at great speed.

The milk float hadn't even come to a stop before the lads jumped off, wading in to the Barr Estate mob with fists and boots flying everywhere. Harry and I, in the general melee that ensued, both got knocked through the privet hedge into the neighbour's garden.

With us both re-emerging a moment later, Harry having got his left shoe embedded up a plastic gnomes arse, we both just stood there in amazement, watching the action unfold. I saw the Bull Mastiff throwing punches, until Eddie finally sorted the ugly one out with a head butt and down he went. With the ring leader now down on his arse, and after more bloodletting, the Barr Estate mob soon realised they were outnumbered and outmatched, receiving more than they were giving, so they quickly backed off and retreated. Eddie, still fired up and still going forward, shouted, 'Now piss off you lot, keep well away from here and in future stick to your own patch, you bunch of tossers.'

The Barr Estate gang scurried off licking their wounds, and the dairy lads gathered round us, dusting themselves down, still running high on doses of adrenalin, a couple of them with bloody noses, but that didn't seem to matter them they were all so fired up. Harry and I were still shaking; especially Harrys left leg, as he eventually shook the garden gnome off his shoe.

'Listen, Eddie,' said Harry. 'We can't thank you guys enough, we were going to be in for a right old beating, we owe you a lot, mate, really we owe you a lot.'

'Harry's right, Eddie,' I added. 'We owe you big time.'

'Yes you do, so if there's another church dance, I get to dance with Moira first.'

'Eddie, what are mates for? I'm sure that could be arranged.'

Eddie just laughed. 'You're my mates, and anyway my lads are tough bastards and always up for a scrap. It's being out in all weathers on our job, I guess it hardens them up.'

Harry and I thanked Eddie's mates and they climbed back on to the milk float and took off back to the dairy, shouting and repeating, 'We are the Dairy Boys and we are the best...' Well we had to agree with that.

We could see Mr Richards standing in the doorway of the store. He put up his thumb as a sign of recognition of the outcome, and there's no doubt he was so glad his windows were still intact.

With much relief, the drama now over and with our blood pressure returning to near normal, we carried on walking home.

'That was a bit too close for comfort, mate,' I said.

Laughing, Harry said, 'Yes it was, by the way we still haven't talked about our holiday plans.'

'No,' I replied, and I too started to laugh. 'I can't stop thinking about you and the garden gnome.'

'Ha, ha. Don't you dare mention that to anyone. I hope the neighbour whose garden it was didn't see us. His hedge certainly took a battering.'

'You can trust me, anyway. I don't feel like talking about holidays now. Why don't you come round to my house one of the nights next week and we will get it sorted? I will ring you.'

'Right, ok, sounds good to me.'

So after a very eventful weekend to say the least, and with much relief, we both went home.

Chapter 5

Arrived at work on Monday morning still sporting my war wounds. I couldn't wait to tell Russell about the weekend events, especially my time with Moira and the fight at the dance.

Russell, who had already arrived early for a change, was bragging to someone in the general office of his latest sexual conquest over the weekend. No doubt it was with the blonde girl from the offices over the road.

'Morning, Russell,' I said. 'What was that I heard you talking about, could it have been the office girl over the road by chance?'

'Oh, hi,' replied Russell. 'Yes, I was just saying what a good time I had with my date, Debra, and yes you're right, it was my blonde bit of stuff from the offices over the road, who incidentally,' he said, laughing, 'was certainly a blonde all over!'

'What do you mean blonde all over? I don't understand.'

Russell replied, still laughing, 'The beaver matched as well.'

It took me a minute to come up to speed on that one before saying, 'You know, you really are over the top, mate, rude to say the least. Anyway I don't know how you can get so intimate on a first date.'

'You've either got it or you haven't,' said Russell. 'Anyway what the fuck has happened to you, mate, don't tell me you walked into a door or something.'

I was about to explain to Russell when Mr Cooper the office manager came in and stood before us, the bottom button on his waistcoat undone, this due to his potbelly, and looking at us over the top of his thin rimmed glasses. He pointed to both of us and requested that perhaps Russell and I would like to join him in his office. We looked at each other, both realising that a stern telling off, or even possible sackings, was imminent, this obviously relating to our problem with the dumbwaiter.

A telling off we duly got from Mr Cooper, stating that any more stupidity like this and we would both be getting our cards. He went on to explain that Sid was now off sick, probably through stress, and this was in no doubt partly down to us two, pratting about. He continued that we would have to give the trolley dollies extra help until he was back. 'Unless of course you want to tell your fellow workers they won't be getting any tea today.' Mr Cooper continued saying, 'By the look of your face, Alfie you have also been in some sort of scrape over the weekend, and it's certainly not a good look to have in the office. Your general conduct is in question.' But with half a smile he continued, 'I hope you weren't on the losing end.' And at that we left his office, winked at each other and proceeded to get on with our jobs.

The week at work progressed without further incident, quite the norm in fact, except for everyone wanting to know how I'd got my bruises. Mr 'Trump' Thompson was doing his usual bit and Barry Thorn at the other end of the office, chatting up anyone wearing a skirt. I arranged for Harry to come round to my house on Friday night to discuss our summer holiday. With only two weeks to go until the factory industrial fortnight started, the time of year when most people take their holidays, we needed to get something sorted out before there was no accommodation left.

Friday night soon came round and Harry, having finished work at the store, came round as arranged. Mom suggested that we should use the front room to discuss our plans.

'Would you like a piece of cake with your cup of tea?' Mom asked Harry.

'Oh, yes please,' said Harry.

'I asked Harry where he would like to go, if he had any preferences.'

'I don't mind, really, but it needs to be a resort where we can have some fun. A good beach is essential with a long promenade and a funfair, plus a theatre where we can see a show, if you know what I mean.'

'Yes I do, I'm up for the same sort of thing really. Mom has suggested Blackpool or Margate but I'm not keen on them, although they both have funfairs.'

At this, Mom came in with the drinks and her homemade cake, saying to us that she'd been listening to our conversation and had another idea as to where we can go, that's got everything we want.

'How about going to Great Yarmouth?' she said. 'It's supposed to be a lively place with a great beach and they do have a long promenade. There's also a theatre. In fact I think they have two and before you ask a "funfair" too.'

I turned to Harry, saying, 'What do you think about going there then?'

'Well sounds good to me but we need to know how far it is and how long it will take us to get there in the van. You know how sluggish the old van is.'

At that, Dad came in, having heard our conversation also, saying, 'Great Yarmouth is on the east coast, about 200 miles from here. That's about seven to eight gallons of petrol, and with petrol at over three shillings a gallon it will cost you a fair bit to get there and it would take you all day. That's pre-supposing of course that the van will get there.'

'If they can send a chimp into space, I'm sure we can get ourselves to Great Yarmouth, Dad.'

Dad laughed and walked off, giving the rental TV a thump on the top with his fist as he passed by, stopping the picture from rolling.

'That's a long way isn't it?' said Harry. 'Dad's van may not make it. It's getting old and has done loads of miles, however, Dad did say we could use it and that he would get it serviced and checked over for us before we go, so it should be ok.'

'That's brilliant, and don't take any notice of my dad. He's used to travelling on a train or charabanc when they go on holiday. He makes you laugh really, because he can't drive anyway. How's this for an idea? We could break the journey up, go so far and kip in the back of the van overnight. We could put in a mattress and even take a primus stove to make hot drinks and bacon butties for our breakfast.'

'That sounds ok. It would be less strain on the engine as well,' said Harry, 'and it would be an adventure for us.'

That idea went down well with everybody except Dad, whose cherished primus stove, which he uses when he goes fishing, we would have to borrow.

Mom said, 'What are you going to do about your accommodation when you get there? Do you want me to take a look now in the Daltons Weekly for somewhere to stay, perhaps a bed and breakfast place? You would be better off knowing you have a place to stay, rather than going on spec, especially being the industrial fortnight.'

Harry said that the Daltons Weekly sold well in the store; it's a good source for finding out things, not only for holiday accommodation, but also if you wanted to buy something second-hand, like a lawn mower, that's if you wanted one.

'Well we don't need a lawn mower, you tit, so yes Mom, if you could take a look down the accommodation column that would be great.'

Mom started to look down the listings for all the bed and breakfast places situated in Great Yarmouth.

'Here you are,' said Mom. 'There's a place listed here that says it has comfortable rooms with washing facilities, I suppose they mean bathrooms, and it comes with a breakfast. It also has a drinks licence, not that I agree with you having too much alcohol.'

Dad buts in with, 'Yes, that doesn't mean you can get pissed every night.'

'No, Dad. What's the name of it, Mom, and what do they charge for a week's stay?'

'It's called "Selbourne House". Sounds rather posh doesn't it? I would have to ring them to find out if they have any vacancies first for the date you want to go, plus what they would charge for a double room.'

'What do you think, Harry, shall we go for it? perhaps the first week in August I think.'

'Why not?' replied Harry. 'We have to get something booked up. We could start out a day earlier and do what you mentioned and stay overnight in the van, it would be great fun.'

Mom said she would give them a ring straightaway,

see if they have any accommodation left and book it if it's a reasonable price. This was easy for Mom to do, now that we have a phone in the house. We could hear Mother on the phone in the other room, speaking in her not-so-good posh voice, asking questions, until eventually coming back into the room and wearing a smile, telling us that we were booked in for a week's stay at the Selbourne House guest house, and more importantly it was only four pounds ten shillings for the week, including breakfast.

Harry thanked Mom for booking it up and then turned to me, saying, 'That's great, we will also need to buy some new holiday clothes as well.'

'That's right; I need new trousers and some casual shoes.'

Our holiday was at last finally settled, and it was also payday that day, so Harry and I could go into town tomorrow and get our holiday shopping underway.

Chapter 6

Met up with Harry on Saturday morning, who had been given a rare morning off work by his dad, and we caught the 42 bus into town to do our shopping. We sat up top on the bus, chatting about the various clothes shops we should visit, eventually getting off the bus in Union Street to make our way along Corporation Street; there we would make a start. I love the buzz of the city centre on a Saturday, everyone scurrying round in and out of the various shops, everyone looking for the weekend bargains. Women wheeling push chairs with their screaming kids in tow, wanting sweets or ices on sticks. The street vendors ply their wares, offering the latest bargain of one sort or other. For a few pennies you can buy a cone of baked potatoes, which with a sprinkling of salt goes down well. The newspaper sellers on the street corners, shouting the title of their papers in the usual abbreviated format. People know what they mean though, when they shout for instance, 'Spatch a Mal' for the Despatch and Mail. The market stalls are full of colour, displaying fruit and vegetables with the cries from the sales people offering today's deal. The only thing I don't like is seeing the fish stalls, displaying all sorts of fish lying on marble slabs, especially the ugly ones with their glazed eyes and mouths wide open. Crabs the size of dinner plates, although I've never been one for sucking the meat out of a crabs claw and I don't know how anyone can eat the jellied eels they also have on display.

'Alfie, where shall we go first then? I need to look at jackets and I'm in need of a pair of trousers, adding to what I've already got,' said Harry.

'All down to cost, mate, we could go to Burton Tailoring or John Colliers, and there's always Zissman's or maybe Lewis's. Yes, perhaps we should try Lewis's first, they are probably going to be the cheapest.'

'Don't you need a new shirt, Alf?'

'Very funny, as it so happens, Mom got the blood out after several washes in the boiler.'

So, continuing along Corporation Street we arrived at Lewis's, the biggest department store in the city. Entering through the main doors on the ground floor, we decided to use the lift, as the men's department, according to the sign on the wall, is on the fifth floor. Having pressed the call button, we both stood looking up at the arrow pointer on the dial above the lift door. The arrow indicated the lift was on the fourth floor and Harry pressed the brass call button again. Eventually we could hear the lift coming as it rattled its way down, arriving with a jolt. The noisy metal crisscross doors were opened on the inside first, and then the outside ones were also pushed wide open, this was carried out by an old female lift attendant, dressed in a black and white uniform and, given her age, she had probably been doing this job since Adam was a lad.

She stepped out, saying with a scowl on her face, 'I heard you the first time.' We walked in, without saying a word, then the attendant stepped back in and leaned out, checking left and right to see if she had any more customers before closing the outer sliding crisscross door with a bang and then the secondary one, this too with a bang.

I thought; fancy doing her job, day in and day out. We both looked at each other, with Harry whispering to me, 'This is what it must be like if you get banged up in "Alcatraz".

'Yes it is,' said the attendant, obviously having good hearing despite her age, 'And you certainly make sure your fingers are nowhere near the doors, when I pull them to, that's for sure.'

At this the attendant pulled down a little wooden seat and promptly sat down, putting her wrinkly hand on a brass lever ready to kickstart the lift into life. Then, turning to us, she asked, 'Which floor would you like?'

'Menswear,' I said.

The lift started off with the usual jolt as we started to go up, and we were able to look out through the crisscross doors at the various floors as we passed by. Each floor dedicated for different products, such as household goods, haberdashery, ladies fashion etc., until we reached the men's department on the fifth floor. Again the lift stopped with a jolt and then after the same operating ritual by the aged lift attendant she opened the doors. We stepped out at the men's department onto a very shiny linoleum floor, polished no doubt by cleaners every night as they scurry round after closing time.

The floor was well-lit from the daylight coming in from the many windows down the one side, and we slowly made our way down the first aisle looking at the various display cabinets. It was very quiet, with only the occasional cha-ching of a cash register being used and the sound of the cash draw flying open. I saw a sales assistant struggling to spread the fingers of both hands on the till keys, all the time checking to make sure she had got the right keys covered, before pressing them hard down.

'Is that your shoes squeaking I can hear, Harry?'

'No, it's the cheeks of my arse. I'm about to spend money.'

'Didn't think you were a tight arse?'

The smell of new clothes greeted our nostrils as we passed rolls of new suit cloth currently on display. This material you picked if you wanted, as they call it, a made-to-measure suit, but that's not what we were looking for, and anyway it would be out of our price range. It's off-the-peg stuff for us, all ready made up in various sizes, and you just hope they are going to be the right sized fit for you, as opposed to having a tailor-made suit that should fit perfectly. Anyway, from what I can gather, not having an off-the-peg suit but rather having it tailor made for you, even if I wanted one or could afford one, spares the embarrassment when an assistant, when measuring for the trousers, asks 'Which side do you dress, sir,' in other words does your penis remain central or does it fall left or right.

Not knowing where to start, we ambled on, passing the ready-made suits hanging on rails, all in neat rows with their labels attached to the sleeves. We carried on, looking for the jackets and trousers, passing displays of different styles of hats on shelves and highly polished wooden cabinets with glass fronts displaying neck ties, bow ties, socks, scarfs and underwear.

A floor walker, armed with the proverbial tape measure round his neck, suddenly stepped out from behind one of the cabinets, like a tarantula waiting for its prey to enter its lair.

'Can I be of assistance, gentlemen?' he asked, whilst rubbing his hands together and stepping back slightly as he slowly eyed us up and down at the same time.

This floor walker had obviously clocked us coming down and had been lurking, ready and waiting to pounce. A slim-looking bloke, sharp nosed with a pencil moustache, his hair plastered with Brylcreem with a parting down the middle, dressed in a grey suit with the widest lapels going. He continued rubbing his hands together with a certain gaze of uncertainty. He was probably thinking that we were just time wasters, given our ages, and certainly not welcome in his department, but he was going to practice his sales pitch anyway.

'Yes, mate,' said Harry, 'you can help me; I want to try on a jacket.'

The floor walker, still not sure about us, stared at Harry, saying, 'Oh, what sort of jacket would sir like? Single breasted, double breasted, short or long, vented or non-vented, grey, blue or brown, check or plain? Your size would help too, sir.'

Harry, I could see, took a moment, no doubt thinking that this little prick thought we hadn't got a chamber pot to piss in and couldn't afford to buy anything, this borne out by the way he was constantly looking us up and down.

I thought the bloke was taking the piss too; he wanted too much bloody information for my liking, I let Harry deal with him.

'Listen, mate, I've come in for a suit jacket, not a lecture and I don't need it on the never-never either, I can pay for it. I just want a normal two button jacket in blue,' said Harry in an agitated manner, 'It also needs to be at the right price too, nothing too expensive.'

The floor walker took a further step back, eyeing Harry up and down yet again, and in doing so decided he must be a 38-inch chest and reached down a blue single-breasted jacket, non-vented.

'Would sir like to try on this one?' he said, as he removed the hanger and held it up for Harry to see and slip on.

I was now inwardly laughing at Harry because I know he doesn't like the cut of this bloke's jib at all. He would tell him it's not what he's looking for and within a couple of minutes we would be getting ourselves out of there. As the floorwalker held the jacket open for him to try on, Harry turned, sliding his arms backwards into the sleeves, and at the same time he looked at me and winked. The fit was drastically bad, the sleeves were too short and as Harry turned back round too much material in the back, and knowing Harry as I do it was not really his style anyway.

Harry caught my eye as I shook my head slowly from side to side in complete disgust at the way the jacket fitted. Even the style and cut of the jacket was not nice. Harry winked at me again, then looked at the floorwalker and said what do you think? The floorwalker said. 'I think its suits you just fine, sir, just fine.' Although the floorwalker was a lying bastard, Harry amazingly said to him, 'I will take it, but I will need a pair of trousers, a shirt, shoes, a tie and a pair of these here cufflinks that you have in the display cabinet.'

I stood there in disbelief as to what Harry was saying, and not surprisingly the floorwalker had by now completely changed his attitude and was giving Harry his undivided attention.

Half an hour went by with Harry trying on clothes and picking colours, none of which were suitable, with no guidance from the floorwalker except to say 'Suits you, sir.' I just looked on, wondering what the hell was going on, knowing full well that he was not even able to pay for all this clobber anyway. By now the assistant's counter was covered in all the items Harry had agreed on.

'Is that everything then, sir,' said the floorwalker, still rubbing his hands together, and by now other assistants looked on in awe, wishing they too had a customer spending money like this.

'Yes thanks, I think that's it, but would you remove all the price tags for me and wrap them up,' said Harry, to the floorwalker.

'Certainly, sir,' he replied, thinking of his pending sales commission.

Harry glanced round and smiles at me.

Meanwhile I was starting to fidget, pacing up and down, my eyes looking everywhere else, rather anxiously wondering what the hell was going to happen next. What was Harry up to?

As the floorwalker removed all the tags and continued wrapping everything up in the usual brown paper, Harry said to the man, 'It's very quiet in the department at the moment isn't it? You don't seem to have many customers today.'

Harry turned to me and gives me his third wink before turning back to hear the assistant's answer.

'Yes, it's a bit quiet,' said the floorwalker, as he busily wrapped up the last item, 'but I'm sure we will have a good day's trading as the day progresses.'

'Well,' said Harry, leaning forward and slapping both his hands flat down on the counter, eyeballing the assistant, 'your day is about to go downhill fast, mate, because you can put all the price tags back on this lot and stick everything right up your arse where the sun doesn't shine, you condescending little prick.' The floorwalker was left stunned and open mouthed as he stood behind the counter completely motionless.

Harry quickly turned and grabs my arm saying, 'Come on, mate, we're off.' We both moved at a very fast walking pace towards the lift, but decided under the circumstances that a quick exit was needed and that the stairwell was a better bet. At that we broke into running mode with all eyes on us. Our feet didn't touch the floor as we both headed for the exit, barging through the double doors to charge down the five flights of stairs. My heart was racing away after bolting down the first flight of steps, and at this point we heard the security alarm bells ringing and loud voices echoing down the stairwell, both of us now hoping that we would make it outside before the security staff felt our collar.

'You bastard, you could have warned me,' I said to Harry, as we raced down the next flight of stairs two at a time. Shouting could be heard up top, the banging of doors being opened and the sound of footsteps on the stone staircase getting louder and louder.

I looked over the handrail and could now see more security on their way up, we were about to get sandwiched. I grabbed Harry's arm after descending the next flight of stairs and pulled him through the doors to the haberdashery. Running down an aisle to find the next stairwell, I knocked over a huge display of cotton reels and rolls of ribbons, leaving them rolling all over the place in my wake; that should slow them up a bit. At last another stairwell presented itself and we carried on going down, two steps at a time, to get out. Reaching the lower ground floor we were through the exit doors in a flash and out onto the street with great relief, probably only just in time as well.

The streets were now much busier, which helped as we

dodged our way past people, trying to put as much space between us and Lewis's.

'I can't believe what's just happened,' I said, as we continued to half walk and half run at the same time down Corporation Street, hoping to get people and some distance between us and Lewis's. Both still looking over our shoulders, checking behind, to see if we were being followed by some burly security guard in size fourteens.

'Well he really pissed me off,' said Harry. 'He was devious and would have sold me anything for a quick sale.'

As we slowed down to a walking pace, mingling in with other shoppers, allowing us to get our breath back, I was still looking back over my shoulders at times, just in case Lewis's security were still following.

We started to calm down and went down Union Street, finding ourselves outside Zissman's tailoring.

A Jewish shop I thought, in the Dale End quarter and a much smaller store, so we'd try this store first, see what they had to offer. I had used Zissman's before; they only cater for men. In fact, the jacket I wore to the church dance without a collar, now splattered with blood, I bought that from there.

We stood outside taking a gander through the window at the tailor's dummies, hoping something on the display might be what we are looking for. The dummies had no heads or feet, just the torso, but hopefully displaying the latest trends for the season.

'See anything that you like, Harry?'

'Well I'm not thinking of anything other than a jacket, something like that,' he said as he pointed to one of the dummy's wearing a dark blue blazer. 'That could look pretty cool with a pair of grey slacks, what do you think?'

'Yes, I could go for that, but don't you think one of us should have something different?'

'Possibly, a different colour maybe, let's just go in and take a look, try a few things on. We may not be impressed with the way it looks or the fit when we try it on.'

'Fine, mate, but don't get doing what you did to that poor bloke in the last place, even if he was a little shit.'

'He deserved it. Let's go in and see what's what. I'll behave this time, and anyway I'm knackered after that last episode.'

As we entered, there was a totally different atmosphere in this store; it had a much better feel about the place somehow, smaller and more personal with a warm welcoming smell about it. As we gazed around, some chap was already being helped with trying on a suit. Very low music was coming from a speaker on one of the shelves, probably wired up to a valve set in the back room; it was 'Wonderful land' by the Shadows. Just nice background music.

In this store the garments were all on rails against the walls with a few tables in the centre of the room displaying jumpers and shirts. Shoes were stacked waist high in their boxes on one wall, displaying the actual shoe on the top box, all very neat I thought. Again a floorwalker approached us, but this time he simply said, 'Hello lads, what can I do you for?' This was certainly a change from the last place! Despite his phrase 'do you for', we would need a fair deal that's for sure.

Harry opened up with, 'We both want to try on the blazer that you've got on display in the window. It's the one in dark blue, to the right of the window.'

'I know which one,' said the sales assistant. 'That's a new line that's come in this week.'

This guy, I think, was possibly only a few years older than us and was wearing a smart pin-striped suit and tie to match. Somehow you get that good feeling in some places, and this time, hopefully, we were going to relate to this bloke and get fitted out for our summer break.

Harry tried the jacket on first, raising his shoulders up to stand tall, his hand stroking the left sleeve, feeling the material as though he was stroking a Persian cat.

'Feels nice,' he said. 'How is the fit, Alf?'

But before I could answer the assistant jumped in with, 'It's looking a little short; what you need is a regular size,' and he reached up for another jacket, using a pole with a hook on the end, he lifted the hanger and coat down. We definitely knew now that we had the right person here serving us. He was not trying to stich us up like the last bloke, and he didn't even have the proverbial tape measure round his neck.

'He's right, Harry, you needed the regular one.' Turning to the assistant I said 'You can get one down for me as well, mate, to try on; I'm also a thirty-eight-inch chest and a regular fit as well. We are a similar build, well, almost.'

'In the same colour, too?' asked the assistant. 'Oh, by the way,' he added, 'please call me Ted.'

'Yes, the same, why not,' I said. 'We are mates after all, and I like the colour, we might as well look like twins I guess.'

Whilst we both stood admiring ourselves in the mirror, we noticed the assistant, Ted, had disappeared.

'Alf, I'm happy with this if you are,' said Harry.

'Yes I am, fits me well too and I like the shiny metal buttons.'

At this, Ted reappeared, presumably from the stock room,

with two pairs of mid-grey slim-fit trousers over his arm.

'These trousers are thirty-two-inch waists, they will go well with the blazers, lads. Worn with a white shirt, you will both look the business.'

'You know what, Harry, Ted can read my mind; I said to you that grey trousers would work well.'

'You didn't say that, I did.'

'Well it doesn't matter who said it, let's see if they fit.'

'Use the changing rooms, go and try them on. I've given you sizes that should be just right.'

Well, in no time at all we emerged out of the changing rooms, both standing ogling ourselves again in the full-length mirrors. Giggling like a couple of excited girls fresh out of puberty.

'Well, mate,' I said to Harry, as we both stood there, twin like, 'if these outfits don't impress the girls on holiday nothing will.'

Looking round, I noticed that Ted had disappeared yet again into the back.

Harry said, 'He's in and out like a dog at the fair, but so helpful.'

Ted returned with two pairs of shoes in his hands, saying, 'These are what you need to finish off your outfits, they are very smart, comfortable, with leather soles and uppers and as you can see they have stitched detailing, take a look and see what you think.'

We both turned round to see him holding very smart white slip on moccasin shoes.

'I took a guess and brought you a pair of size nine each, if you both sit down I will find a shoehorn.'

We just looked at each other in amazement, and after trying on the shoes I quietly said to Harry, 'This bloke is good, and although he is doing a right selling job on us, that's ok, but only if we can get a deal out of him.'

The assistant was great and had matched up our outfits just perfectly, it was just the cost, and I wasn't sure if I had enough money on me to pay for it

'Ok Ted, if we have all this clobber, are you going to give us a deal or what?' said Harry.

At this Ted pondered for a moment, smiled and said, 'Look lads, on Monday we are having a sale that will give you ten per cent off, so why don't you reserve them, come in Monday to pay for them, then you'll get the discount, if you think that helps you.'

'Too right mate, it does.' Thinking at the same time it gives us the time to borrow any money from our parents that we might need.

'Harry, I could pick them up in my lunch hour on Monday and bring them home after finishing work.'

So the assistant totted up what the items would cost after the discount and wrote it down for us.

'Perfect, Ted,' said Harry, looking at the figure.

'Alf, I will get the money to you tomorrow; I will get a sub off my dad if I'm short.'

'Well get a big sub if you can, because I might just need to borrow a bit as well.'

Having sorted that out, we thanked Ted for his help and gave him some details and he agreed to have them wrapped up ready for Monday lunch. We came out well chuffed with our purchases, glad that we didn't have to do more shopping around and happy with the way we had been treated at Zissman's. We were now spent out and not wanting to stay in the city any longer, so we caught the bus home.

Chapter 7

Another week at work was rolling by, with Russell and me keeping our heads down, getting on with our work as normal, just in case Mr Cooper was still keeping his beady eye on us. We continued as well, much to our annoyance, to do our duty after the tea break in clearing everything away. However, it did allow me to have my usual chat with the lovely Miss Marshall, who said I was looking a lot more like myself after the fight. The girls in the typing pool, who had been very sympathetic towards me, had placed their empty cups neatly on the tray for me to collect. One of the girls said I was also looking a lot better now the swelling on my face was going down, and another, smiling, suggested that she could rub it better for me. Red faced with that remark, I left the typing pool gathering up the rest of the cups.

The weekend soon came round and with just a week now before we go away on our Holly Pollys, Harry and I met up and decided, now that the van had been checked over, we should try it out and put a few things in the back, starting with a small mattress, rugs and a few cushions. He also wanted to buy Lynda the latest Elvis Presley record called 'Return to Sender' as a going away present.

We began to sort the van out, deciding that if we hurried

up we could get to Taylors record shop before it closed for the day. Taylors is a record store where you can go into one of the sound booths at the back of the shop, put on the earphones and the assistant will play the record of your choice, you then listen to it before you actually buy it. Sometimes, even when I'm merrily penniless, I listen to a number of records and then tell the assistant I can't make up my mind and will call back later.

Having made the interior of the back of the van comfortable we drove to Taylors and went inside. 'I hope Jenny is serving,' said Harry. 'She will normally let us listen to more than one song if the store is not too busy.' Jenny is a lovely good-looking girl, with a smile to match, nice figure too. The shop was not too busy, and because Jenny was serving we listened to not only Elvis's song, but also the new one from the Tornados called 'Telstar', which sounded futuristic. We finished off with 'Twistin the Night Away' by Sam Cooke.

Harry purchased the Elvis record he wanted, having parted with 6s/8d, and we left and got back in the van.

'Alf, why don't we ask Lynda and Moira if they want to go for a ride out with us tonight?' said Harry, reaching into the back, connecting the wires up to the spare battery to test that the radio was still working. On hearing the sound of the Everly Brothers singing 'Wake up little Susie', we knew the battery was ok.

'Good idea, yes a bloody good idea, I may be able to have a smooch and a fumble with Moira. God. if ever there was ever an inconvenient moment it was the night of the church dance when the fighting broke out.'

'I'm talking about going for a ride round, Alf, not you shagging in the back whilst Lynda and I are up front and yours truly doing the driving.'

'It's ok for you, Harry, you are sexually active. I could do with losing my virginity before we go on holiday. I don't want to be in a situation where I'm not in control and look stupid. I also think that Moira could show me a thing or two. At first I thought she was a little shy but I now know differently, I think she wants it as much as I do.'

'Oh yes! How do you know that?' said Harry.

'Let's just say it was all action the last time we met, the shop was open and ready to deliver. Moira was by no means shy and in fact quite up for it. Well she was, before the shit hit the fan.'

'Why, are you so bent on having sex anyway?'

'Because having a healthy sex life is important for your general wellbeing.'

'Who the hell told you that?'

'No one, I read it in a book.'

'A fucking book, oh right, it had to be a fucking book. Your mom's *Woman's Weekly* no doubt.

'Well, I suppose if they do want to come we can explain why we won't be around next week and see if we can keep them sweet until our return. My Elvis record I bought for Lynda might help.'

Harry knocked on Lynda's door whilst I sat in the van. I saw Mr Evans, Lynda's father, open the door and say something to Harry. He followed that with a look over Harry's shoulder at me in the van. Then Mr Evans closed the door and Harry returned back to the van.

'He's just pissed me off,' Harry said, as he got back in the van. 'Apparently he knows about the problem at the dance and is not happy that his daughter was involved in what was my problem. But as I said to him, it was us two that got a kicking and it's now been sorted and wouldn't happen again. Anyway, Lynda wasn't in, she's with Moira at her house. Do you happen to know where she lives, Alf?'

'Yes, up by the Beacon in one of the posh houses that have recently been built.'

'Do you know the house number?'

'No, but when we had a chat that time in Lyn's house she said it was a detached house, on a corner, with a bright red door, so let's drive up there and see if we can find them.'

We slowly drove up Beacon View drive, looking for a house with a red door, only to find out that all the houses had bright red doors. Obviously a posh area, probably a load of stuck up bastards that copy each other. However, one of the houses at the end of the road, I noticed, had a light on in an upstairs bedroom window and Harry stopped the van outside. The window was open and even sitting in the van, with the engine clattering away, we could hear music blaring out with the sound of Bobby Vee singing 'Take good care of my baby'. We sat just listening to the radio for a moment, feeling sure that this had to be the house.

Sure enough, as we sat there twiddling our thumbs, two girls appeared in the window. We were at the right house alright, and we could see Lynda and Moira in the bedroom jiving to the sound of the music. That's the best of being a girl, you can dance with your own sex and nobody cares.

'Alf, you go and knock on the door this time and see if they want to come out for a drive round,' said Harry.

'Ok, but what if someone else comes to the door, especially her father?'

'Well I wouldn't ask him if he would like to take a ride …

Just ask to speak to Moira and don't forget to say please.'

This I did, and after knocking the door a couple of times, the problem being the loud music, a woman answered the door; I guessed it was Moira's mother straight away, so I smiled and gave my name, asking if I could please have a word with Moira. Looking over her shoulder, the woman, still holding the front door open, bellowed up the stairs, like a fish woman in the market place.

'Moira … Moira, someone here to see you.' Not once but several times, because of the loud music playing,

Eventually Moira heard her mother calling above the sound of the music, and having switched off the record player came to the top of the stairs.

Looking down over the bannister, she said, 'Mom, what do you want?'

'There's someone here at the door to see you.'

'Who is it?'

'I don't know.' Turning back to me she asked my name.

'It's Alfie, Moira, now just get yourself down here and deal with it. You'd best come in,' she said to me.

Moira came down the stairs and upon seeing me said, 'Hello, I wasn't expecting to see you.'

With her mother still waiting in the wings and me not thinking right, I said, 'Would you and Lynda like to come out for a quick ride with me and Harry?' expecting her mother straight away to jump in and say no to that request. Instead, she said 'Bloody great. Yes you can go out; we can then have some peace from that pop music blaring out all the time.'

Lynda had also at this point come down into the hall.

Turning to Moira, her mother said, 'You two can go out,

but I want you back by ten pm, you know what your dad's like.'

The girls quickly grabbed their coats and we left to pile into the van, Harry and Lynda in the front and Moira and I jumping in the back.

'Where are we going for a ride then?' said Moira.

'Well we can't go far, it's gone eight o-clock now,' replied Harry

Lynda jumped in saying, 'Let's just park up at the Beacon and listen to radio Luxembourg; we will have more time and it will be quicker to drive us back home.'

Sitting in the back on the mattress with Moira, I was not going to argue with that request, so Harry made a quick left turn and we very soon headed up the road that would take us to the top of the Beacon.

It's a hill on green belt land with a war memorial on the top. There are parking spaces on each side of the road and the view is spectacular. At night the lights glitter in the distance from all the buildings and you can see the car headlights as they move down the carriageways. We managed to find a parking space and Harry switched on the radio with the sound of Ray Charles singing 'I Can't Stop Loving You'. A great song to play as Harry by now had his arm around Lynda and, much to her surprise, gave her the record he had bought, and they then snuggled down up the front and began talking quietly. Before I knew it Moira had thrown a rug over us and we too settled down on the mattress. Moira was certainly not slow at going forward and was kissing me with real intent. The smell of her body was fresh with the fragrance of a recent soapy bath, and it was not long before I threw caution to the wind, irrespective of the company up front, and started with a snogging session.

It was now getting dark and the temperature outside had dropped. With our warm bodies, the front windows of the van were misting up, so with no windows in the back this was surely going to be my moment. Moira by now was partially undressed, except for her skirt, and she unbuttoned my shirt, pulling it out of my trousers. Our naked bodies touched. How fabulous that feeling was, a feeling I should have had the pleasure of much sooner. Quiet intimacy with a passion was about to take place with Moira starting to guide me to that most joyous of joyous places.

Suddenly the moment was interrupted with someone or something banging on the side of the van. Startled, we all sat up quicker than you could say Jack Robinson and I looked at Harry, saying, 'What the fuck was that?' With another bang on the driver's door, a torch light shone through the side window, lighting up Harry's face. Harry quickly adjusted his clothing and wound down the driver's window saying, 'Get that light off me, what's all the banging about?'

The torch light moved and shone onto us two in the back. Moira quickly covered up and I moved forward a little, and once I had got past the dew drop on the end of the nose at the window, I could then see whoever it was had a helmet on and a uniform.

'What's the matter, officer?' said Harry. 'What's all the commotion about?'

'Just checking who's who. We've had a report of a man here on the Beacon, going round dressed in just a Mac, flashing his private parts. A woman walking her dog has been traumatised by it and is very upset, so I'm doing a check on all the vehicles up here and want to know who is in them and what they are up to.'

'That's as may be,' said Harry. 'Frankly you startled us, banging on the side of the van like that. Anyway, we are only listening to the radio, officer; you can get good reception up here on the Beacon. I don't possess a Mac and certainly don't go round flashing my dick; neither does my mate, although he hasn't got much to flash anyway.'

'Wrong,' whispered Moira from the back. 'I'll be the judge of that.'

Turning to me to me, she said, 'It's just perfect, and one bloody day you may get to prove it.' We quickly got dressed under the rug and, having done so, both showed our faces up front. The policeman shone his torch away from us. Obviously deciding that we were not of interest to him, he apologised and walked away.

'Can you believe that?' said Harry, winding up his window. 'Banging the side of the van like that, typical of authority, but at least he apologised.'

'I can believe it,' I said. 'It's the story of my life at the moment, mate.' Thinking that it was the second time Moira had taken me in hand at a crucial time, and still to no avail; close again but no cigar as they say.

'Ok lads,' said Lynda 'let's go home anyway. It's getting late and I promised to be home on time.'

'Right,' said Harry, and we left to drop the girls back home.

As we said our goodbyes, Harry gave Lynda a kiss and she thanked him for the record. It was evident that Lynda and Harry were now becoming an item. Certainly the girls, I think, were feeling a little sad at not coming on holiday with us, but tried not to show it.

I kissed Moira also and whispered the words, 'One day we'll

get it together. It won't be long before we are back off holiday. It's only for a week and when I do get back, we will spend as much time together as we can. Perhaps we can go to the pictures.'

Chapter 8

The week at work went by very quickly and without any hassle; Mr Cooper being away on holiday meant everyone was more relaxed and in a good mood. Russell had now turned his sexual desires towards our Jane Brown in the drawing office, the one with the pointy tits. Yesterday, he had a bit of a set to with Barry Thorn over her, which ended up with Russell pinning Barry to the wall by the stationary cupboard, telling him to back off chasing Jane or his wife might just find out what he's been getting up to. Typical of Russell, but not surprising, he's a bit of a rocker and not someone to be messed with. Any one that can ride a Norton Dominator motor bike, with its size and weight, can handle himself,

Friday night soon came round and Harry and I started to get into the holiday mood straight away, first by filling up the van's petrol tank at the local garage. Then back in the yard, we began to load up the van with our gear through the rear doors. We loaded essential items that we would need for the journey last, including Dad's primus stove, a small frying pan, bottles of beer, a pack of Park Drive cigarettes – not that we smoke much, it just makes us look and feel older. Dad's vintage hurricane lamp went in, that we've had in my family for many years, apparently; it'll be handy for the night time stop over.

Plus our two suitcases, shoes, a couple of blankets and our new jackets, deciding to hang them up separately so as not to get them too creased.

Harry said, looking in the back of the van at the amount of stuff we had put in, 'How are we going to sleep in there?'

'Stop worrying, we'll manage. It's only for one night, some stuff can come out and be slung under the van. If you can't get much sleep, you can play catch up when we get to Selbourne House.'

Harry and I studied the road map next and, allowing for the fact that the van is in no way a flying machine, decided that the stopover has to be about halfway between here and Great Yarmouth.

'Alf, I think, looking at the map, the stopover should be, barring any breakdowns, at a place called Huntingdon.'

'That's fine with me, Harry; all we need to do is park up on the side of the road somewhere, a grass verge maybe, take on a few drinks and crash out. Then in the morning I will cook breakfast and then we carry on – Bob's your uncle and Fanny's your aunt.'

I arrived at the store's back yard quite early the next morning with a box of food Mom had put together, which Harry found a space for in the van, next to the beers. Mr Richards told us that the van had better come back in one piece, and we were not to drink and drive. Having had that warning we set off. So, finally after all the chitchat we were on our way at last, with Harry driving to start with and me getting comfortable in the passenger seat, not that the van is that comfortable, a bit of a bone shaker really. In fact it's no racing machine either, that's for sure, with only three forward gears. We have a nickname for it, we call it a 'Rolls Can Hardly'. It rolls down the hills, but can hardly get up them. However, we made steady progress throughout the day, listening on and off to any radio station, in between losing the signal that is. Our conversations were always about girls, what type we liked, big girls, slim ones, tall or short, and were we likely to meet a couple that are also on holiday, and more importantly looking for sex.

'Do you think Lynda might be the one you want to go out steady with?' I said to Harry. 'I know, in the main we are all just good friends, but she really is a nice girl and I think she likes you a lot, mate.'

'Do you know what, Alf, she is the one who, strangely enough, I have never tried it on with. Yes, we have a smooch, and at times it gets a bit heated, but then the friendship side of it kicks in. It's probably because we were school friends initially. But who knows what the future might bring. If I'm eager to get back and see her, perhaps then I will know.'

At that, with Harry continuing to press on, crunching the gears every so often, I opened a couple of beers I had stashed up front and searched for the crisps, along with the bottle opener.

'Why is it, Harry, when you look for the usual little twist packet of salt they put in the bag, it's nearly always at the bottom of the fucking bag? Why Smiths Crisps can't put it in the bag last is beyond me.' At that my bottle of beer tipped over.

'You can clean that up. I don't want to get the van all messed up before we've even got there,' said Harry.

'Stop worrying, I'm sorting it. What time was it when we started off? I'm trying to work out what time it will be when we get to our overnight stop.'

'It was about nine o'clock I think, when we eventually set off.

The problem is having to stop every so often to let the engine cool down for a while. We have been doing between thirty to fifty miles an hour, depending on whether we are going down or uphill, but the van's still plodding on and that's the main thing, we've done about ninety miles so far.'

'Well on that basis it's going to be around five o'clock when we get to somewhere near Huntingdon. That's about half an hour from now, but we need to pull over before then as I'm in need of a slash.'

Harry pulled over into a lay-by and we got out, stretched our legs and relieved ourselves, watering the hedgerow as you do, still talking about the need to find our overnight stop as soon as possible before we start losing the light. We continued our journey and it wasn't long before we passed a sign saying Huntingdon. We drove on through the village and back out into open countryside, looking for a suitable place to park up and spend the night.

'Alfie, there's a wide grass area coming up. Could be a good place to stop.'

'Ok with me, mate.'

So Harry pulled off the main road and on to the grass verge, continuing straight through a gap in the hedge and on to a field the other side. The van bounced around as we drove down a farm track, turning off onto a level grassed area, at the bottom of a hill.

'I wondered for a moment where you were taking us, Harry. Anyway, here looks as good a place as anywhere and there's someone else camped up there,' pointing to the very top of the rise.

Harry pulled on the handbrake and looking up the hill said,

'Yes, I can see what looks like a van, and they've got a camp fire on the go too, so I guess it's ok to stop here overnight.'

'Yes I agree, we'll park here for the night, keep our distance. Whoever it is up there might know the farmer and has had permission to camp here overnight.'

'Well we haven't got permission, but we will just have to pack up and drive on if it's a problem.'

'That's fine with me,' I said, jumping out. 'I'm just about ready for a couple of drinks and a bite to eat.'

We opened the back doors of the van, looked in and decided it was best to sort a few things out straight away for the evening sleepover. We emptied some stuff out on to the grass either side of the van, this left enough room for us to climb in and sleep later. We did this as the sun was going down and the daylight slowly faded. You could feel a summer chill in the air as Harry and I quickly finished sorting things out. We foraged round in the back of the van for the food that Mom had prepared for us, grabbed a few beers for us to sip, threw a rug down and sat down on the grass, relaxing as we talked about the rest of tomorrow's journey whilst eating our sandwiches and drinking. Harry decided he would drive first for a bit and then change over when we have a stop for me to drive the rest of the way.

'You know, Alf, whoever is sitting up there on the top has got that camp fire absolutely raging. It's lighting up the whole of the camp area and I can see someone with long hair.'

'Has to be a woman then?'

'May be, whoever it is, they keep looking down at us and waving their arms about,' replied Harry. 'Perhaps they are praying to their god whilst doing a fire dance or something.'

'We're not in the wild west, Harry.'

'Actually, I don't think it's a woman, looks like a man with long hair and possibly a beard to match, and I don't think it's a van he's got parked up by the hedge either. But I can't quite make it out, can you see what it is?'

I looked up again, saying, 'Well I agree it's certainly not a van. They don't make vans with a rounded roof like that, and I think there are steps going up the back of it.'

We carried on munching our sandwiches and broke out another couple of beers, both of us still looking, from time to time, up the hill at this character.

'Wait a minute; I think there's a horse up there too,' I said.

'Yes it is a horse, I can see it now with the light of the fire. It's just poked its head out from behind whatever it is that's parked up there.'

Looking up again, Harry continued, 'I know what that is, it's a travelling caravan. He would be a "Romani Jones" character.'

'What does that mean, "Romani Jones"?' I replied.

'A "Romani Jones" is slang term, otherwise known as a "Gypsy", or a "Tinker".'

'Oh, I know what you mean, an Irish traveller.'

'That's right, but don't look now, he's up on his feet and starting to walk down towards us.'

'What's he coming down to us for?'

'How the hell should I know?'

'I don't want any aggro, I'm on my holidays.'

'Stop worrying,' said Harry. 'Let's just relax, carry on as we are. Anyway, whoever it is probably just wants to ask or tell us something. It might be important.'

'I'll tell him something important, if he starts,' I replied.

The man, unsteady on his feet, stopped halfway down the

hill and beckoned to us again, as if he wanted us to go up to him. We didn't move a muscle, and after a few seconds he again continued walking down, in our direction, swaying somewhat from side to side as he did so. Harry said he thought the guy looked as though he'd had one sherbet too many.

As this guy approached us, not liking the situation, I reached out for the van's engine cranking handle, something we keep inside for starting the engine if the battery goes flat, and tucked it under a coat lying on the grass, just in case.

As the swaying bearded man approached, I could see he was most certainly a Gypsy, dressed in a pair of well-creased baggy black trousers that were tucked into his brown calf high boots that had string for laces. He had a grey shirt on that was probably once white with the sleeves rolled up and a black leather waistcoat. A red bandana adorned his forehead, disappearing behind his straggly long grey hair.

'Hello, my fellow travellers,' the man said, in a soft Irish accent, as he stood before us. We didn't say anything, as he slowly straightened himself up. He was six foot two if he was an inch, tattoos on his arms and wearing earrings.

'Nice old van you've got there, lads,' the Gypsy said, as his eyes surveyed us and everything around us in the flash of an eye. 'I like your hurricane lamp too, that's an old one, make no mistake. Yes a fine old lamp that's for sure.'

Harry looked at me, I looked at Harry, both thinking that he was possibly about to rob us or do something rather unpleasant. My hand slipped further under my coat, gripping the starting handle even harder, and I broke the silence saying, 'My mate and I, we're on a week's holiday and heading for Great Yarmouth in the morning, thought we would park up here for the night.' I paused for a moment, thinking, if there is going to be a problem let's find out what it is now. 'Is there a problem?' I said, 'We don't want any trouble, mate.'

'No trouble, lads, no trouble at all, just being friendly to my fellow travellers.'

'What about you then?' I continued. 'Are you on holiday or on your way somewhere?'

The Gypsy answered with, 'I'm always on the way to somewhere, matey, but I've been camped up here for quite a while now and the farmer hasn't bothered me.'

I thought, that's not surprising, given the size of him, and, like us, I guess the farmer doesn't want any trouble. The Gypsy, who had by now squatted down in front of us said, 'Typical of you English, to be sure, your only pleasure is crammed into just one or two week's holiday a year. You should be like me, on holiday all year round, be a free spirit with a Gypsy soul and find inner peace. I go where I like, when I like, always camping under the starry night sky, come rain or shine. It's a wild life, but it's how I like it.'

There was a moment of silence after that, us thinking he's got to be on something or other. The Gypsy continued with: 'To be sure, we all have a little free spirited Gypsy in us, just waiting to get out. I'm a friendly foe, lads, so don't just sit here on your own boys. I've got good stuff to drink and a fire to keep us warm under the starry night sky and plenty of tales to tell. So join me, come up to my camp and sit a spell. We can exchange meaningful words, don't you think so, lads?'

Harry, as my hand slowly released its grip on the starting handle, looked at me, saying, 'That's an invitation that I like to hear,' then turned to the Gypsy and said, 'Yes sure, we would love to come up to your camp. We'll just finish off here and be with you shortly.'

At that the Gypsy, unable to get himself up from his squat position, rolled over and used his hands to push himself up to the kneeling position. He then, with some difficulty, stood up, paused for a moment and slapped his hands together as he prepared himself to make his way back up the hill. As he did so he was still swaying from side to side, making it heavy going as he made his way back up the hill to his camp.

'Harry, you've accepted his invitation and we don't really know who he is or what he's like. He could be spinning us a yarn, nice on the outside and a wandering lunatic on the inside really, just look at the size of him.'

'Stop worrying, the taller they are, the harder they fall.'

'Yeah right, but if he is a nutter, I'm gone.'

Having sorted the inside of the van out for the night's sleep over, I lit the hurricane lamp and hung it up on the outside of the van, a guiding light you might say, for when we come back down, later in the dark. We secured the van to make our way up the hill and join our Gypsy friend. The sun by now was so low in the sky shadows lengthened by the minute, and having accepted his invitation, rightly or wrongly, both of us being very unsure as to what we might encounter, we set off up the hill to his camp.

We approached his colourful caravan with its rounded roof. Wooden steps led up to the front door which had a window in it with its curtains closed. The sides of the caravan were gaily decorated with bold black and gold markings, finished off with white spoked wheels and black hubs. I noticed that a lot of the Gypsy's possessions were straddled all around the place; he had obviously been camped here for quite some time. There were working tools, leather harnesses, ropes, wicker chairs, bowls, buckets, log piles and strung out between two trees his washing, which looked as though it had been hanging there for days. Alarmingly, I noticed what appeared to be a double-barrelled shotgun leaning up against one of the wheels of the caravan. Unsure, I elbowed Harry in the ribs, and nodded towards the gun, 'Check that out, that's a gun isn't it?' I said.

Harry momentarily stopped in his tracks, looked at it and then looked back at me, shrugged his shoulders, and said, 'It's definitely a gun, but don't worry, we'll be alright. There's two of us.'

'Yes, but he's got the fuckin gun, with two barrels,' I said, as we slowly walked on into his camp.

The Gypsy was sat in front of the fire, both hands covering his face; I wasn't at all sure if we should be doing this, and one thing's for sure, we'd be going down the hill faster than we came up.

'We stood before him, and after clearing my throat loudly I said, 'Hello, my name's Alfie and this is my mate, Harry. What's your name?'

The Gypsy, dropped his hands and with his bloodshot eyes now wide open looked up and replied, 'Silvanus.'

Harry said, 'Silvanus, that's an unusual name.'

'I suppose it is,' he said, 'Silvanus. It's mythological and refers to the Roman tree god.'

'Is that why you have camped here under this tree?' I said, laughing.

A cold shiver came over me as I suddenly wondered if my remark may not have been appropriate, and hoped he hadn't taken offence by it. Fortunately, Silvanus smiled and then laughed and coughed at the same time, showing his discoloured teeth with a solitary gold tooth at the front.

'Being camped under the tree has nothing to do with it. It's only you English fools that camp at the bottom of a hill, where the ground can be very damp and much worse if the heavens open up. The high ground is much better. Now squat yourselves down, lads, and take a drink with me.'

We immediately sat down on the wooden stools he had placed by the fire, like kids in the classroom, not wanting to offend this heavily built guy in any way. His dark complexion was highlighted by the flickering fire, showing his well-lived-in face, presumably from years of living outdoors, I guess, with the sun beating down, lashings of rain and high winds. The elements have certainly taken its toll on him, resulting in his weather-beaten face. He had what looked like battle scars on both his cheeks, and the tattoos on his forearms arms depicted women with headdresses on, jewellery and heavy make-up. As people have tattoos for one reason or another, no doubt his tattoos had some sort of deep meaning for him.

'Your tattoos look great,' Harry said. 'Very colourful, and I notice they are both of women.'

'Gypsy women are known for being of strong will; it depicts how the women in their traditional garb would have looked centuries ago, and represents the nomadic Gypsy way of life, my way of life.'

At that Silvanus got up to reach out three pewter-looking mugs from a box attached to the side of his caravan, and came back to sit down on a large, old looking leather travel trunk, framed with brass and handles to match. He placed the mugs down on an upturned wooden box in front of us and began to pour out what I thought was wine from some sort of thick leather jug. Silvanus filled up the mugs nearly to the top. Then, looking at us with his searching eyes, he proceeded to pull out a large knife from the inside of his right boot and lay it down on the box in front of us. The blade of the knife, which must have been at least eight inches long, curled up to a point at one end. The blade, pointing in my direction, glistened in the fire light and most certainly would make a mess of you, if used in anger.

What's happening here? I thought, as I immediately recognised it as being a Bowie knife, the likes of which my father would never have let me have, 'What do you want with a hunting knife round here?' he would say.

Silvanus has a need for it, though, pulling it out and placing it so prominently in front of us. I had the feeling something was going to happen. We could hardly just get up and run off like little kids having broken somebody's window playing football.

Harry and I just sat there, staring at the knife for a moment, cautiously waiting, both of us gripping the stools we sat on. We nervously watched as the Gypsy rose again, picked up the knife, grinned and placed it back down on the box. Then, reaching to a bag behind him, he took out something wrapped in a muslin cloth, sat back down and carefully unwrapped a block of cheese. Using his knife, he cut off a few chunks of cheese, handing pieces to us on the pointed end of his Bowie knife. His use of the knife was now much to our relief.

The colour returned to our cheeks as we both sat there, munching our cheese, whilst Silvanus this time stuck the knife in the box and gave us a mug each and then raised his to offer a toast, saying, 'May a mouse never leave your meal bag with a tear in its eye.'

The three of us raised our mugs and all took a drink at the same time. I suddenly felt a warm glow inside as this drink travelled down, real slow like. It was like nectar, certainly powerful stuff. As Harry and I then tucked back into the cheese, Silvanus filled up his own mug straight away, I was amazed as to how he could drink this fire water so quickly. No wonder he swayed around the way he did when he walked.

Harry looked at me after taking a few more sips of his drink and whispered, 'Is your throat on fire? This is some powerful stuff we're drinking.' I was unable to answer for a moment, the drink having taken my breath away, so I just nodded and grinned like a Cheshire cat. Whatever the drink was, it certainly brought some colour to our cheeks. We both had the warmest of feelings inside and now, feeling more relaxed, we held out our mugs for a top up, just like a couple of kids wanting more of the amber nectar.

'I like your caravan, Silvanus. It's bright and colourful, nicely decorated,' said Harry. 'How long have you had it?'

At this the Gypsy looked up and banged his mug down, on the box, saying rather displeasingly, 'First of all, it's not a caravan.'

'Oh right ... well, wagon then,' continued Harry.

'Wrong again. You English, you know nothing.'

Silvanus paused for a moment before continuing with, 'Well, to be fair, you are partly right. We call it a Bow-top Vardo, it's from the Iranian word "Vurdon", and it's been in my family for many years. It was handed down to me by my father and now it's mine to look after. In fact, my father still travels in it. It's my monument on wheels.'

Harry, puzzled, thought about what Silvanus had just said

and followed it up with, 'Is your father here then? I've not seen him about. Is he asleep in the Vardo?'

We were in a staring contest for a moment before Silvanus reached across, put his hand on Harry's shoulder, shuffled even closer on his trunk to eyeball him and said with his Dragon breath, 'I'm sitting on him.' He patted the side of the leather-covered trunk, then laughed out loud whilst leaning back and taking another drink of his fire water.

Having heard this, my eyes moved away from Silvanus for a moment and back to the fire, watching the sparks go up with the smoke into the night sky and thinking, did I hear that right? Did he say his father was in the trunk? What the hell have we both got ourselves into?

Looking back to Harry, who in turn looked at me, both unnerved at what Silvanus had just said, we slowly stood up at the same time, wondering if he was a murderer, having bumped off his old man or something. Or could it just be the ramblings of a drunken Gypsy? Either way a quick exit down the hill was going to be needed.

'Sit down, boys,' Silvanus shouted. 'Sit down and relax, don't be alarmed about my father; he's been reduced to ashes. When he died, his ashes were sealed in a wooden casket and I keep them in this trunk, it pleases me, because he travels everywhere with me. As I said, it's my monument on wheels.'

At that we were both yet again so relieved and sat back down to sip our drinks.

'Sorry,' I said. 'We thought for a moment that you had, I mean, that you had ...'

'Silvanus,' piped in Harry, rather quickly, 'what Alfie is trying to say is, did your father die of old age or something else?'

'Actually, he didn't die of old age, although he was getting on a bit. No, he was a bare-knuckle fighter and had one fight too many and died.'

Silvanus turned away and stared into the flickering fire, no doubt thinking of his father. 'He had a big send-off though, with the clans coming from far and wide to pay their respects.' Patting the side of the trunk again, he continued, 'I like to think he's still with me, as I travel around the country.'

Harry and I, now having relaxed, drank more of his fire water before I quickly changed the subject and asked Silvanus how many miles in a day he might travel.

'Ten to fifteen miles. It all depends on old big boy there,' replied Silvanus, referring to his horse, which was still moving about at the back of the Vardo.

Harry asked Silvanus if he was ever scared of being outdoors at night, being alone and all that, perhaps in some of the more remote places.

'I was born into this life and I like it, not because it's easy but because it's hard, and I can take care of myself, so being on my own is not a problem.'

'Is that why you have a gun? For protection, in case someone wants to harm you?'

I was thinking why did Harry have to bring up the subject of the gun for Christ's sake?

'Lads,' continued Silvanus, 'people with any sense should not be thinking of harming a Gypsy. Killing one of us, or perhaps cutting one of us up, say, into ten little pieces, would not be a good idea. Word would be out far and wide and then you get ten more gypsies to deal with, yes to be sure. Anyway I use the gun to shoot rabbits for food and the foxes for fun.'

I could see his horse moving about in the inky darkness, tethered to a metal stake in the ground as he munched away in his nosebag. I asked Silvanus what the name of his horse was, to which he replied. 'The big man, he has many names, especially when things don't go right for instance, but his favourite name is "Oh Come On", he jokingly added. 'Patch is his name, he's fourteen hands and has a mind of his own at times, but he always keeps me on the right track.'

'Patch, that's a good name,' Harry said.

We carried on drinking the fire water that Silvanus somehow kept an unending supply of. A lot of banter ensued over the next couple of hours, Silvanus at one point reaching out a tin box, revealing what looked like tobacco, together with cigarette papers. He sprinkled whatever it was from his tin box on to the paper and started to roll it into a cigarette shape.

'What sorts of cigarettes do you boys smoke?' asked Silvanus.

I replied with, 'Park Drive, or sometimes a Strand. The Strand in the main, probably, because I like the TV advert –"You're never alone with a Strand".'

'I don't buy packet cigarettes; I like to roll my own. Would you boys like to try one of these?' Silvanus picked up some more tobacco with his fingers and sprinkled it on to the paper, before licking it and rolling it together. 'These are very special tobacco leaves that a friend of mine grows,' he continued, as he rolled another one.

I declined, but Harry, who by now was well on the way with the wine drinking, said, 'Sure, I would like to try one of those.'

Leaving them to it, I got up and went to see old Patch, as the effects of the wine by now had given me enough Dutch courage to go near him.

'Your right, Silvanus, he's a big horse. What breed is it?' I said, as I gave him a pat down.

'He's a piebald cob,' said Silvanus.

'Travellers always seem to have multi coloured horses, don't they, Why is that?'

'It's a breed we have had for hundreds of years; piebald cobs have a pattern of coloured splotches on a white coat. Or you can have a skewbald, which has white splotches on a brown or black coat.'

'Oh right,' I said, well you learn something new every day, not really taking all that in but fully understanding why he called him Patch.

At that I could see Harry was starting to be in the land of the fairies, singing and rambling on to himself, so I thought it was time to call it a night and get him back to the van before he had any more wine or drew again on that cigarette. I don't know for sure what they were both smoking, but I guessed it might be Wacky Backy.

'Silvanus, we've had a great night,' I said. 'Thanks for the cheese and wine, but it's time for us to be on our way. We have another long drive on our hands in the morning and it's getting quite late.'

'Do you need a hand with Harry?' replied Silvanus. 'It's going to be quite dark on the way down.'

'No it's ok, I can get him back down the hill, thanks. It's not far to go and we've left a light on.' The way Silvanus swayed around he'd be no bloody use anyway.

'Ah! The light from your fine old hurricane lamp no doubt,' said Silvanus.

'Yes, that's right.'

At that I got Harry, who had slid off his stool, up on his feet and put his one arm round my shoulder. After thanking Silvanus again, we started to head on down the hill, staggering all the way, stopping only to have a piss in the hedgerow. We arrived back at the van and the light from the lamp certainly helped us as I opened up the back doors and got Harry, who was still rambling, inside and settled him down for the night. I closed the back doors and threw a blanket over the two of us and crashed out.

Chapter 9

I woke up the following morning staring at the roof lining in the van; the air in the van was foul, a mixture of Wacky Backy, booze and Harry's bowels. I rolled over and could see that he was still out for the count, obviously still comatose from the night before. I edged my way to the back of the van and flung open the rear doors to let some fresh air in. I filled my lungs up with the fresh morning air, thinking it was a good job I wasn't feeling too bad after last night's session with our Gypsy friend, especially as Harry had lost it completely, I needed to be able to cook our breakfast this morning; I was looking forward to cooking in the open air.

A lovely day it was too, with the early-morning sunshine filtering through the trees, the smell of the dew on the grass and the dawn chorus in full swing. How nice it was to be in the open countryside, being part of nature you might say. Harry was still buried under the blanket as I slid out of the back of the van and did a full stretch, taking in more of this fabulous morning. Looking up the hill I was amazed to see that our Gypsy friend had gone, lock stock and barrel. No horse, no Vardo and no Silvanus in sight.

'Harry,' I shouted, 'Silvanus has gone, he's hitched up and pissed off.'

Harry, stirring by now, rolled over and uttered, 'Probably gone for more wine.'

'No you idiot he's left, moved on, buggered off, done a bunk, vanished during the night I guess.'

At that Harry threw the blanket off and sat up, only to groan whilst holding his head, before slumping back down again.

'Oh! My head hurts. It hurts so much; it feels like it's been split with an axe, and my mouth tastes like a Turkish wrestler's jock strap. What a time we had last night, the Gypsy turned out to be a really nice bloke, don't you think? In fact very generous, and there's us, both thinking he might have been some sort of rogue, thug or even at one stage a murderer.'

'Well you certainly took advantage of his hospitality, mate. I had to carry you back last night. You were well pissed, high on something or other, possibly the wine or more likely the Wacky Backy. I think you and our friend might have been smoking pot. Fortunately the lamp I left hanging on the side of the van helped to guide us back down the hill, and that reminds me, I need to turn it off.'

'Don't bother,' said Harry, 'I will do it. I need some fresh air, it stinks in here. I'll take it down; I need to work this hangover off. I've got the drums of the loudest symphony playing in my head at the moment.'

Harry edged to the back of the van. 'I bet it's out of kerosene by now anyway.'

'Right, you do that and I will sort the van out inside, now that the air has cleared. I need to get organised for breakfast; the way you're feeling it's obvious you're not good for much else this morning.' Harry stumbled out of the van and looked for the lamp, first the one side and then the other.

'Where did you hang it, Alf? I can't see it.'

'It's hanging on the roof rail on the side of the van, you idiot. Get a grip, mate, you're still obviously under the influence.'

'Alf, Wacky Backy or no Wacky Backy, it's not there now. I can't see it, its fucking gone, mate.'

I jumped out of the van and looked for myself and sure enough, it wasn't where I had hung it. I had to think for a minute, in case I'd got it wrong.

'I put it right up there, I know I did. Some bastard has taken it.'

'That bastard is Silvanus,' Harry replied. 'You can bet it's him, he's had it away during the night. If you remember, when he first came down here to talk to us, he took a liking for it, saying how nice it was.'

'Yes, I remember, he decided to nick it sometime during the night. No wonder he's taken off in a hurry, the crafty bastard.'

'Well even if he was still here I doubt we would have challenged him, especially him being armed with a gun and lord knows what else in his arsenal.'

'His knife would have put me off.'

I carried on with the job of preparing breakfast, getting out a little table, the primus stove for making tea and a ground sheet, etc. Harry connected up the radio to the sound of Bobby Darin singing 'Mack the Knife' which, I thought, was rather apt. It made me think of our thieving Gypsy friend, although, his teeth were far from being pearly white and he certainly didn't keep his Bowie knife out of sight.

I got the food box out Mom had prepared for us and I asked Harry if he could eat a bacon and egg sandwich if I cooked it.

'Is the Pope catholic?' he replied. 'Alf, you cook it and I will eat it. A few drinks are not going to spoil my first morning on holiday; anyway I'm feeling a bit better now.'

'Yes, that's because your brain is now less fuddled with the Wacky Backy.'

The smell of the bacon and eggs cooking outdoors was fantastic; it gave us both an appetite. Harry, looking over my shoulder said, 'Crisp it up a bit for me.'

'Yes, Your Lordship. It will be cooked in a minute or two, so you get the primus stove going afterwards and make the tea whilst I make the sandwiches. After covering our now burnt bacon sarnie with a dollop of brown sauce, converting it into something we could actually eat, we both relaxed back into the holiday mood whilst eating breakfast.

'Harry, how many sugars have you put in that cup?'

'Three.'

'That's yours then, I only want two in mine.'

After enjoying a hearty breakfast we cleaned up and loaded our things back into the van, and because Harry was still feeling a little fragile I decided to drive the rest of the way to Great Yarmouth. Obviously the Wacky Backy may be clear in his head, but it would certainly still be in his blood stream. I topped up the van's radiator with some water we were carrying, checked the oil level, and with the sound of Brenda Lee singing 'I'm Sorry' we set off to continue our journey to Great Yarmouth.

'That song's rather apt, don't you think,' said Harry. 'Do you think it could well be a message over the airways from Silvanus? Perhaps he's feeling remorseful for stealing our lamp?' We looked at each other and laughed, both saying together, 'No fucking way.'

Our encounter the night before with our Gypsy friend, who undoubtedly was now the proud owner of our lamp, was all we talked about for the next few miles. Then Harry settled down reading a copy of the *New Musical Express* which, I noticed, had a photograph of Elvis Presley on its front cover.

It was now midday and it wasn't long before we were on the outskirts of Great Yarmouth. Harry asked me if I had the address of the place where we were staying.

'The Daltons Weekly is under your seat. Mom has put a sheet of paper inside with all the details on it, the name of the place where we are stopping and the address.'

'Well I know its Selbourne House,' said Harry

'Yes I know that, but take it out, we are nearly there. The house number will be on it. It may be that we have to park up somewhere and take a walk round to find it first.'

Harry reached under the seat and got out the information. 'We want Howard Street North, apparently, and it's in the centre of the town. Within minutes we were driving into the resort area and heading downhill and on to the sea front.

'I saw the sea first,' shouted Harry, 'that's something I used to say as a kid.'

'I still am a kid,' I said, 'when it comes to the seaside.'

We drove along the road adjacent to the long promenade, but being at the seaside is one thing, it was girls we were on the lookout for.

Driving slowly along with the beach on our left, all the buildings on the right were mostly hotels or bed and breakfast places, but I noticed a couple of bars too that had tables outside so you could look out over the sea whilst having a drink.

'Alf, one of the places I've noticed called "Paddy's Bar" looks a good one, they too have seating out front, so we could give it a try later, if you like.'

'Yes, that's fine with me.' I dropped the window down to smell the sea air; finally we were at the seaside, away from the hustle and bustle of everyday life.

The promenade was packed with holidaymakers of all ages walking along in the sunshine, many with their kids in tow, ice cream in one hand and a bucket and spade in the other. As we drove further along the road we could see that the tide was well in and bathers were having a good time paddling, some with the proverbial car tyre inner tube, having fun floating around on them. Family groups were scattered all over the beach as we drove up towards the Britannia Pier. Other holidaymakers were relaxing as they sat in gaily coloured striped deck chairs that lined the railings on the promenade, taking in the views. There were lots of people strolling along on the pier too. Fishermen could be seen at the end of the pier, with their rods and kids with crab lines.

'Wind your window down, Harry; fill yourself up with some of this sea air.'

As we were passing the pier, I looked at the billboard at the front entrance and stopped the van for a moment.

'Harry, look who's appearing at the theatre on the end of the pier,' I said, pointing at the billboard. 'Tommy Bruce, Mike Sarne, Joe Brown, Ricky Valance, they are all brilliant.'

'Yes I see, but there's also another theatre in the town called the Windmill, so we need to see who's appearing on there too. Look, there are amusements on the pier as well. Don't drive off for a minute, I want to take all this in.'

We sat in the van with the engine ticking over, glad to be at the seaside, watching the scene unfold around us. At that a group of girls, arm in arm, dressed up in their summer clothes, came strutting their stuff down the promenade towards us. As they started to walk by, Harry wasted no time and stuck his head out of the window.

'Hi girls,' Harry shouted, 'hang on a minute, don't walk on, I need to ask you something.' The four girls in the group stopped for a moment, turned, smiled and slowly approached us, gathering round the van door.

'Are you here on holiday, girls, or do you live in the town?' asked Harry.

'You've got a gob full of questions, haven't you?' said one of the girls to Harry.

'Yes, and you've got a gob full of chewing gum.'

They were all good-looking girls with very developed assets, but two stood out straight away, probably because they were the ones with the short skirts and tight tops. The tallest one of them with the short white skirt and lilac flowery top answered Harry with, 'No boys, we don't live here, and yes we're on holiday. Arrived late yesterday and having a look round for the moment.'

'Well my name's Harry and this is my mate Alfie. We've only just arrived as well and here for the week. We might see you around.'

I leaned across Harry to take a look and as I did so, the girls started to titter amongst themselves, followed by the tall one saying to me, 'You don't look old enough to drive.'

The titter broke into laughter from all four of them, and for a split second her remark took me back a bit, but I didn't take offence.

'I'm old enough for lots of things. Anyway, what's your name? As my mate said, we just might see you around and if you're lucky,' I said with a wink. 'Give you a ride in the back of the van, if you know what I mean.'

'My name is Joan, you cheeky bugger. This is Ruby,' she said, pointing to the one who was constantly chewing gum. Looking to her right she said, 'This is Mavis and her friend Sandra, Sandra being the other one, with a short skirt and tight jumper.'

'Well girls,' said Harry, 'it's been great talking to you but, having only just arrived, we still need to get to our accommodation and check in, boasting, we're staying at Selbourne House. Hopefully we will see you over the holiday. How long did you say you were here for?'

The tall one, Joan, said 'Hopefully for the week, so as you say, we might just see you around, if we've a mind to.'

'Oh, I've a mind to,' said Harry.

I just laughed and said, 'Well girls, we'll look out for you and perhaps have a drink or two, you lot buying your own drinks of course, so hope to see you later.' We left them and continued a leisurely drive further along the promenade.

'Alf, they were a bit of alright and could be up for it. I think one of them could well make your day and give you your non-virginal badge'

'Ha, Ha,' I replied. 'They may not be loose girls at all.'

'Don't you be so sure. I think, the tall one, Joan quite fancies you.'

'Fancies me?'

'Yes, she was checking you out, mate, checking whether you were old enough. I should have said to her that you've had no fucking experience at all and that you would be a waste of a good night out.'

'Very funny, how old do you think she is then?'

'I reckon she is a bit older than the others, probably nineteen to twenty.'

'You know what; I think you could be right, she does look more mature, especially compared to the one chewing gum. For now, though, we need to be on the lookout for street names, mate, and get settled into our digs.'

We came to the end of the promenade and decided to turn round and head back down towards the pier again and turn off into the town area.

'Look,' said Harry, as we turned off the promenade, 'there's a fish and chip shop and I'm starving, pull over into this side street and I will get two portions, we can sit and eat them out of the paper in the van.' This we did and, after filling our faces, I jumped out of the van to ask a bloke who was passing by where Howard Street North was.

'Did he know where it was?' Harry asked, as I jumped back in the van.

'Yes, we have got to carry on up this street and go past St George's Gardens and immediately turn right. Follow the road round and Howard Street is on the left.'

'Brilliant,' said Harry. 'I can't wait to throw our suitcases into our room, freshen up and go out for a pint.'

We arrived in Howard Street and drove along looking for Selbourne House. I noticed that all the buildings in this street were big old three-storey terrace-type town houses. The one house at the end looked double fronted with long narrow windows and a canopy over the doorway.

'I bet that's it at the end of the street,' I said.

As we got up to it Harry looked up, saying, 'Yes this is it. "Selbourne House". There's a sign above the canopy.' So we stopped and parked the van right outside.

Time was marching on so we got cracking and opened the

back door of the van, reached out our suitcases and walked up the two steps to a hefty old front door that was slightly ajar. Pushing it wide open we walked into a small reception area at the start of a long hallway. An ornate chandelier hung directly above us. The hall had a black and white tiled floor with some kind of Turkish rug on it and the tiles continued down the hallway leading to a staircase that went off to the left. Also to the left of us was what looked like a sliding glass window built into the wall. Wood panelling lined the rest of the walls, making it quite dark, lit only with a couple of shaded wall lamps that didn't match the chandelier. At the end of the hall, on the back wall, hung a huge mirror in a heavy frame. This had curtains either side, giving it a window effect. The front room to the right of us has tables and chairs; the tables had white cloths on, so we guessed this was obviously the dining room.

Harry looked at me and said, 'It's a bit oldie worldly isn't it?'

Upon which two men came down the hallway and pushed past us, on their way out to the street. 'Don't mind us,' shouted Harry.

At that, suddenly the glass window panel on the left slid across with a bang, a woman of some age appeared, dressed in black with a white turban-like scarf on her head. The woman said in a very gruff manner, 'What do you two want? You're a bit young to be in here.'

Before we had a chance to reply, a chap came in and pushed past us, saying at the same time to this woman, 'Hello, Tina is expecting me.'

To this the woman replied, 'Yes ok,' and reached to a board with lots of keys on it, took one down, gave it to the man and said, 'Carry on,' followed by, 'It's room six today.' The man walked off down the hall clutching his key and the woman looked back at us saying, 'So, now what is it that you two want?'

Harry replied, 'We have a holiday booking for a week.'

I followed up with, 'It's in the name of Alfie Miller, and this is my mate Harry Richards. My mother booked it a few weeks ago, and sent you a money postal order as the deposit for our stay. '

The woman's attitude suddenly changed, and now smiling she said, 'Oh! Sorry boys I thought you wanted something else. Right then, now let me see.' She studies a book she fetched out from under the counter. 'Ah! Yes, Miller, a bedroom with two single beds for a week, that's right. Remember, there is still a balance of money to pay and this has to be paid the day before you leave.'

'Alf, you're the money man, remember to pay Mrs ...?' Harry looked for a response.

'My name's Mrs Riley, and by the way, I don't want any of that "Old Mother Riley" stuff. You need to pay the balance on Friday, boys, plus any extras. Breakfast is at seven thirty until eight thirty and the front door is shut at eleven thirty. Wait there whilst I come round and I will take you up to your room.'

As we waited for Mrs Riley, another man came in and went straight upstairs.

'I tell you what, Alf, this place is like Grand Central Station.'

'Yes I agree, but if a place is busy, it normally means it's good.'

Mrs Riley came round with a key in her hand and said, 'Ok boys, follow me.'

I was still wondering what she meant by extras. A newspaper maybe. We followed her down the hall to the staircase and started up. It went up one flight then turned up a second and onto a landing. Here hung a picture of a half-naked woman, lying on a chaise lounge. That's something you don't normally see in a guest house, I thought. We went past a couple of doors, and in an alcove I noticed that there was a sink with brass taps, a mirror on the wall and a pendant light hanging above it. Mrs Riley pointed out that this was a washing facility and was in addition to the jug and hand bowel in our bedroom, adding that there was also a bathroom on the top floor, next to the lounge, but that's first come first served. Moving further along the landing, the floorboards creaked under the well-worn carpet until Mrs Riley stopped and opened a door and pointed out the communal lavatory. She stopped outside a door with number three on it.

'This is your bedroom for the week, lads,' she said, and promptly unlocked the door. We walked in and could see that this was the bare bones of a bedroom, showing its varnished wooden floor boards, a rug and two single beds with carpet runners either side. No wardrobe, just a chest of draws with a cream hand bowl and water jug on top, plus a single chair in the corner. One centre light shade, complete with fringe and curtains that were closed at the top and tied to the sides at the bottom. A net curtain covered the bottom half of the window.

'Now, I will tell you two, only my girls are allowed in this house by the way,' said Mrs Riley. 'So you're not allowed to bring any girls back here.'

Strange thing to say, I thought, but perhaps the girls she refers to are her daughters. My only real concern was the fact that I noticed there was only one pillow each, and I like to have two, but before I could ask for another, Mrs Riley quickly walked out the room, closing the door behind her, revealing a metal coat hanger on the back of the door. A hanger in place of a wardrobe perhaps, I was thinking this place was far from being ideal.

Harry turned to me, saying, 'Alf, your mom said this place was described as comfortable accommodation. I'm not sure it is, mate, and quite a busy place as well.'

'I know what you mean. It's not floating my boat either, but Mom would have booked it in good faith.'

'I know that, I'm not blaming your mom. It's just disappointing that's all.'

'Well let's just throw our stuff in for now and go out for a drink. We'll head on back down to the prom so we can get our bearings.'

As we left the room, Harry said, 'There isn't a key to lock the door; Mrs Riley must have taken it back with her, what are we going to do?'

'That's not right is it? Let's put our suitcases under the bed for now and sort it out with Mrs Riley when we go down, I just need that drink.'

Mrs Riley was nowhere to be seen when we got down stairs. We waited for a while and then decided to secure the van and see Mrs Riley later, as by now it had gone seven-o-clock, so we set off to see the sights, finding it still very warm with lots of people strolling along the prom. The cockle stalls were still open and we decided to stop and have some. The assistant, wearing a white coat, was filling up little dishes on the counter and quickly served us a dish each, providing us with a wooden fork. We applied the vinegar, and in my case pepper as well, and stood eating our cockles whilst watching the holidaymakers pass by. Some folks on the beach were still playing in the sea, although at a distance, as by now the tide had gone out and as a result, the smell of the sea air was even more noticeable. We decided to find 'Paddy's Bar', the one that we saw earlier in the day on the way in to the resort. It was great strolling down the prom, seeing the coloured lightbulbs strung in between the lampposts start to come on, as were the lights on the pier.

As we walked past the pier, Harry said, 'Alf, this is where we saw those girls? We must try and meet up with them if we can during the holiday.'

'Yes of course, which one do you fancy then? I bet it's that Sandra.'

Harry continued, 'Do you know what, I don't really mind, after a few drinks I won't much care, shags a shag. Oh, sorry you don't know what that is, do you?'

'Ha ha! Very funny, you just keep having a knock. I will prove you wrong one day. Hopefully I will know by the time this holiday is over, providing I meet the right person.'

'Providing you meet the right person who wants sex, you mean.'

We crossed the road and headed for Paddy's Bar. There were a number of people, young and old alike, sitting outside at tables in the terraced garden area. As we entered, we nodded in general and said hello to an elderly couple who were sat, arm in arm, on a bench at the back, taking in the late sunshine with a drink and both gazing out to sea.

We ordered a couple of brown and milds from the bar and also decided to sit outside. We sat next to the two we saw on the way in, the elderly couple, who were still holding hands. After a while we started to chat to them about the resort. Having told them that we had just arrived that very day and that we had not been to Great Yarmouth before, the man said, 'Mary and

I, we've been coming to this place for years and we've had the same digs for last six years as well. It's like home from home for us.'

He then paused for a moment and followed up with, 'Oh, and by the way my name's Bert, short for Albert, but most call me Bert, and as I said, this is Mary, my wife for the last forty years, bless her.'

Bert, a portly chap with a seasoned drinker's face, a comical looking face in fact, had a certain presence about him. Mary, clutching her handbag and presumably a very devoted wife, said, 'Yes, we first came here on our honeymoon after Bert and I got married.'

'How nice,' said Harry.

Bert, then followed up with, 'We were courting for ten years before we got married, but eventually I plucked up the courage to pop the question to her father. I said to him, can I have your daughter's hand in marriage? To which he replied. "Thank Christ for that, I thought after ten years you were going to ask me for a pension."'

It was a split second before Harry and I realised old Bertie was telling us a joke. Harry and I smiled, giving out a somewhat muffled laugh. Bert himself laughed out loud and continued on with his joke, 'In fact, her father gave me his consent and promised me when we got married he would give me three acres and a cow, and do you know what I'm still waiting for three acres.'

Well that made Harry and I laugh right out loud this time, along with one or two others who were outside dinking and eavesdropping at the same time. Bert was certainly turning out to be a bit of a character.

Mary, his wife, was quick to say, 'Take no notice of Bert,' as she gives him a kick. 'He's always been a bit silly and has been telling Max Miller jokes for years.'

We had a few more drinks and listened to a couple more of Bert's jokes, and then realised the time was now coming up to half-past ten.

It had been a long day for us, and having said our good nights to Mary and Bert, thanking them for a good night, we made our way back along the prom. We didn't want to be late getting back on our first night at Selbourne House. On reaching Howard Street, Harry asked me if I snored, to which I replied no, you won't hear a peep out of me; I was knackered anyway after last night with our Gypsy friend and then driving the rest of the way here.

We arrived at our digs and found to our amazement that the front door was closed, when I tried to push it open, I realised it was also locked.

'Harry, give it another push, it might be just stuck.'

'It's not stuck, its locked. What the hell is going on?' said Harry. 'Old Mother Riley said the door wouldn't be locked until eleven thirty.'

'I'm not sure about this place at all,' I said, as Harry banged on the door with his fist. We waited but no one came, then Harry gave the door a good kicking and suddenly a small inspection flap opened towards the top of the door, with some bloke's nose and his one eye peering through at us.

'What do you two want?' said dead-eyed dick from behind.

I quickly thought that's the second time today we've been asked that question here.

'Listen mate, we would like to come in, if you don't mind,' said Harry.

'If you haven't got an appointment, there's no way you're coming in,' came back the reply.

'An appointment, why in hell's name, do we need an appointment?' said Harry. He looked at me, saying, 'You talk to him.'

'We live here, is what he means. We are stopping here; we're on holiday, booked it and checked in this afternoon with Mrs Riley.' I was getting pissed off by now and continued with, 'It's in the name of Miller, I'm Alfie Miller and I'm not the baker's son.'

'Very funny, you little shit,' came back the reply.

The flap on the door closed to with a bang. We both stood there looking at each other, unsure about our situation or what to do next.

A minute or two later, the door opened and there stood this huge, fat, giant oaf of a man in a dark suit, with trousers that hadn't seen a crease in years. 'I've checked the register,' the oaf said, 'You are booked in, so you can now come in, clever arse.'

'This clever arse would also like a key to our bedroom door; Mrs Riley didn't give us one. Is Mrs Riley about, we need to see her?'

'No,' came back the reply. 'She's out; you will have to see her in the morning.'

With that the oaf closed the door behind us. We walked on down the hall to take the stairs up to our bedroom, and the oaf disappeared into Mrs Riley's office. As we climbed the stairs, we heard music playing and the sound of women's laughter coming from the upstairs rooms.

We reached the landing to our room, and going past the first couple of doors, we heard moaning and groaning coming from inside. 'I hope that's not going on all night,' said Harry.

Closing the door to our bedroom I said, 'Too right, mate, hopefully the other guests will have settled down by midnight. I'm tired now, I'm not going to unpack anything. Let's just put our night clothes on for now and crash out.'

'Yes ok, but I do need to have piss though; I'll be back in a minute.'

Harry used the loo on the landing and coming out he heard noises coming from one of the bedrooms; listening at the bedroom door, he heard music and intermittent moaning and groaning, followed by a muffled scream. Harry quickly moved on when he saw another man coming down the stairs from the upper floor. The man turned and looked at Harry, waited for a moment, buttoned his coat up, then continued on down the stairs. Now what's a bloke doing going out at this time of night? thought Harry, and returned to our bedroom saying, 'There's all sorts of noises coming from these bedrooms, this house is full of strange goings on.'

'What do you mean?' I said, as I got undressed, ready to jump into bed.

'I don't know if some of the guests are just having sex or murdering one another. If you think about it, we've seen a lot of people coming and going, it's all very strange. I can't close these curtains together either, they are tied at the sides, but I don't think anyone can see in from across the street.'

'That's ok; the street lights are not that bright anyway.'

Harry started to get undressed, still complaining about the noises. I pulled back the top cover of my bed, checking the cleanliness of the sheets. There was the odd stain, but I was too tired to worry about it and needed to just crash out. Harry switched the light off, got into his bed and we both quickly fell asleep.

It couldn't have been more than an hour or so later when, in the middle of a dream, I was woken up with the sound of people's voices outside our door, but desperately needing to get a decent night's sleep I rolled over and buried my head under the bed clothes. The voices faded away, but then started again soon after. The voices were of a man and a woman giggling and talking, right outside our door. Still with my head under the bedclothes, and hoping whoever it was would move on down the hallway, I heard the noise of the metal coat hanger on the back of our door rattling and raised my eyes above the top sheet. With the aid of the street lamp I could see the handle on the bedroom door moving and the door opened slowly, letting in rays of light from the landing before bursting wide open. I could make out a man and a woman, silhouetted in the doorway, saying nothing, just swaying from side to side as they peered in.

The man, I quickly noticed, was dressed in a military-style uniform, complete with his sergeant's stripes. Tall and stocky, with his flat cap tilted back on his head, his tie loosened, shirt undone and the woman on his arm, scantily dressed. He stood there with his arm around her waist, holding the woman up, both still swaying slightly back and forth. They had obviously been drinking.

I sat up in bed, saying, 'Who the fuck are you? What do you want?'

He focused on me and in an American accent said, 'Buddy, how long you going to be? Only I need a bedroom right now, the general's up for it!'

Harry, who had also been buried under the bed clothes, but had obviously been quietly listening, quickly sat bolt upright. Now wide awake he threw the bed clothes back and said, 'Look mate, I don't know who you are, but you and your girlfriend can piss off and find yourself another battleground for the night. This is our bedroom.'

This American GI simply kissed the floozy hanging on his arm and said, 'Come on baby let's find a bed in another room, before the general starts his retreat.' Both giggling, they left, banging the door shut behind them.

I turned to Harry and said, 'We need to see Old Mother Riley in the morning and find out what's going on in this place. What with people coming and going, the moaning and groaning, music playing and a drunken Yank trying to turf us out of our beds, it's not right, mate.'

Harry got out of bed and wedged the bedroom chair up against the door handle. 'That will do until the morning.' We both got back into bed, to hopefully get through the rest of the night undisturbed. It wasn't long before we heard voices again and the door handle rattling, but the chair held and with Harry shouting a few choice words it all went quiet.

Chapter 10

Morning came with the sound of seagulls screaming the early-morning wake-up call, telling us to get up and start the day so they could mug us for a few chips. I got out of bed and could see Harry was still gone to the world. I went to the window and drew back the net curtain, letting the sun shine fully through. I looked down on to the street to check and make sure the van was still there, which it was. Looking at my watch, we only had half an hour left before breakfast finished so I punched Harry, telling him to get up, as it was time to get a move on, unless he wanted to miss breakfast. I decided to have a wash in the hand bowl that we had in the room. Harry finally got up to find the bathroom, which he found occupied, and instead of waiting, decided to use the sink on the landing instead.

'I'm not happy with these washing facilities,' said Harry on his return. 'You're trying to have a wash and people are walking past.'

'I'm not happy with the place, full stop,' I replied. 'I think we should go down, have breakfast and decide what to do.'

As we came down the stairs burnt toast filled our nostrils, and as we turned into the hallway we could see the big guy who, eventually, after arguing the toss with him, let us in last night. He was standing on the outside step, like some bloody night club bouncer.

We walked towards him before turning left into the dining room. People were still having their breakfast, mostly women, and very few men. These women, who were sat together in little groups, all turned round and looked at Harry and me as we walked in, acknowledging us with their smiles.

We smiled back and sat at a table laid for two people. Looking round we saw that four of the male guests were dressed in American army uniforms. Harry leaned forward, whispering, 'This place is more like an army barracks rather than a bed and breakfast guest house.'

There was a table with one couple sitting eating their food, which looked like porridge or something; I wasn't quite sure what it was. Another two women sat drinking coffee in between smoking cigarettes. Then a door opened from the kitchen and an elderly woman in a pinafore approached. She had more medals down the front of her pinafore than General Montgomery had won in the war, except her medals were food stains by the look of it, from constantly wiping her fingers down the front of it.

'What would you like for breakfast?' she asked

Harry looked at her saying, 'Do you have a menu?'

'No,' she replied emphatically and then laughed. 'It's either fried stuff or porridge and you need to be quick, it's late.'

I said, 'I would like a poached egg with some bacon and beans, plus a cup of tea please.'

'We don't have cups; it will have to be a mug.'

Harry asked her for a bacon sandwich and tea as well, at which she turned round, disappearing back into the kitchen.

I leaned over and whispered, 'This is not how I thought it would be, we really do need to decide what we are going to do.'

'I agree,' said Harry. 'Let's have breakfast first and then sort it out.'

A moment later a bloke came out of the kitchen, asking if anyone wanted a pint of beer or something a little stronger with their breakfast.

I like a drink, but not at breakfast, that's ridiculous. There were no takers.

At this the old girl rocked up again and slapped the breakfast plates down first, then the drinks.

Harry looked at the bacon sandwich she'd put in front of him. The bread looked very dry, three days old at least, with greasy finger marks on the top, and the bacon stuck out at the ends, curled up like a scorpion's tail. I looked at mine and could see that my undercooked egg was far from being poached and was about to explode its yoke all over the plate. Looking at each other we found it all too disgusting to say the least, so we shoved the plates away from us, took a sip of the stewed tea and left the table.

Having left the dining room, we moved down the hallway a little, out of earshot of the big oaf on the door, deciding on what our next move should be.

'Alf, this is a shithole, mate,' Harry said quietly. 'I don't like it here. The place just isn't good enough to stay here for the week, it will spoil our holiday.'

'You're right; it's not good enough to stay for another night, let alone a week. When Mom booked this place, she wasn't to know, so I'm sorry, mate.'

'No one's to blame, but for now let's go walk about and find a café. I'm starving. We'll get some proper food inside us and plan our next move.'

Having brushed passed the oaf on the door, and after walking round for a while in the town, taking in the early-morning sun, we came across a café called Lilly's right across the road from the Windmill Theatre. We walked in and immediately found the place to be fresh and bright with its orange and white seating, nicely laid tables with placemats and a selection of sauces in the middle. Lots of people were already eating and chatting, which was a good sign. The walls were covered in pictures; I noticed they were all of famous people, singers and actors in the main. We were greeted with a smile by a waitress who said, 'Morning, you can sit anywhere you like, lads, any free table that is, but not the table in the window.'

This we did and, as we pulled out the chairs from under a free table, the waitress left us the menu and said she would take our order in a moment.

'Alf, this is more like it,' said Harry.

'Yes it is. I wonder why we couldn't sit at the table in the window, but no matter.'

The waitress, on returning a moment later with her order pad and pen, asked if we were on holiday. We both replied yes we were, Harry telling her that it was our first morning here really. After looking briefly at the menu, we both ordered a full breakfast, despite not banking on having to pay out extra for our breakfasts. Having both now calmed down a little, we talked about what we were going to do about finding alternative digs.

'Shall we just walk round for now, Alf, because normally guest houses have signs in the front window telling you if they have any vacancies or not. Let's face it, after last night and this morning, anywhere has to be better than Selbourne House.'

'Yes, I agree, Selbourne House is posh in name only and

when we have found another place to stay, we will then decide how we approach Mrs Riley. The problem is getting out with our suitcases, past the big bastard guarding the front door, who always seems to be there.'

'Yes, he's big and scary.'

A woman customer walked over to the jukebox in the corner of the café, pushed a few buttons and made a selection. I watched as the machine selected the chosen record, seemingly from nowhere, and placed it down on the turntable. It was 'The Young Ones' by Cliff Richard, which, at the start of the song, I quietly sang along with …

'That song says it all, Harry. As it so happens, we shouldn't be afraid, worrying about leaving the digs that is. We've done nothing wrong; the place is just not acceptable.'

'No it isn't, not unless you want to pay for sex. It's times like this when we could do with Eddie as back up. He would just step in and hit the big guy, wait until he gets back up and then hit him again.'

'I don't think Eddie's that much of a gentleman.'

'No, you're probably right; he's more likely to put the boot in.'

At that, our waitress, clearing one of the tables close to us, who must have overheard our conversation, came over to us.

'Sorry lads, but I couldn't help overhearing that you were not happy with your holiday accommodation.'

'That's right it's not as we expected. My mother booked it for us. It sounded ok, posh name and all that, but it's far from it.'

Harry piped in with, 'Far from it, it's a spit and sawdust place, that's what it is, and the problem is we've got to find somewhere else for the week and pretty quick too.'

The waitress said, 'Let me bring your food and I will ask my cook if she knows of any place that may have vacancies, she lives in the centre of town.'

'Thanks,' we both answered.

'Sounds promising,' said Harry.

We enjoyed our breakfast, and on that, the cook came over and said, 'I hear you have a problem with your present accommodation. Well the best thing to do is to go to the holiday information centre at the top end of the high street. They are very helpful. They will give you advice and will have details of all the bed and breakfast places that may still have vacancies.'

At that we thanked her, paid the bill with the waitress and said that we would come back to eat there again over the holiday. Little did we know at that time that we would go back to Lilly's café several times over the holiday.

We found ourselves in the high street and entered the holiday information advice centre. After waiting our turn to talk to someone, a guy beckoned us over to his desk and asked us to take a seat. We explained that where we were currently staying wasn't suitable at all, and that we needed to find another bed and breakfast guest house.

The assistant, first of all said, 'Where are you currently staying?'

As soon as I said Selbourne House, he put the pen he was using down, looked up and said, 'Selbourne House?' The person at the next desk gave out a muffled laugh.

'Yes,' replied Harry.

The assistant picked his pen back up, saying, 'You're staying at Selbourne House,' adding, 'You poor souls.' He then called one of his colleagues over and said to her, 'These chaps are staying in Selbourne House.'

Harry and I just looked at each other, both thinking it's obvious people know something about the place, which we don't. The woman he had called over introduced herself as the manager and, taking us both to one side said, 'I'm not surprised you want to move. Selbourne House is the notorious "house of ill repute".'

I turned to Harry and said, 'Is that what I think it is?'

'Yes, a bloody brothel, I guessed it was,' replied Harry.

'That would explain it all then, all those blokes coming and going and the number of women in the breakfast room this morning. Let alone the Yank with his floozy trying to find a bed for the night.'

The woman further explained that the council were aware of what the place was being used for and had been trying to close it down for months.

'Why has that not happened?' said Harry.

The woman told us she thought that it was possibly political, as the place was frequented by the Americans stationed at the RAF base at Kings Lynn further up the coast.

'We can certainly vouch for that,' said Harry.

At that, the manager said she would herself try to help us and called us into her office, saying, 'Sit down, let me have a look at what accommodation may be still available.'

Looking down a list of possibilities from some sort of register, the manager said, 'The guest houses that are registered with us are normally very good. The problem is that July and August is a very busy time and places get booked up quickly. The one place that may be able to help is the "Sea Breeze Guest House" on Nelson Road, run by a Mrs Cassington. She is a very nice person and always tries to help us when we need it. I will give her a ring first, explain the position and see if she has any availability.'

'That would be great if you would,' I said.

The manager then disappeared into another room and closed the door.

'The only problem as I see it,' whispered Harry, 'with a name like Cassington it could be expensive.'

'Do we have a choice? Anyway it's only a bed and breakfast place, not the Ritz, I'm sure it will be reasonable.'

'Well I suppose if they can accommodate us, we can check it out and see if it suits.'

The manager came back after speaking on the phone, saying, 'Mrs Cassington has a room that she keeps normally for her family and doesn't let out, but could be available. She also said that you can have a look at it first, to see if it's at all suitable, and then make a decision. Would you like to do that?'

In desperation we both said yes immediately and the manager gave us the address, saying that it was only a short walk to get to it, also suggesting that if we had only paid a deposit so far at Selbourne House we should grab our stuff and do a runner, leaving the place as soon as possible.

'Can we just run off like that?' I said.

'I don't think for one minute that they will stop you, they will want to keep a low profile, given their reputation.' We both thanked the manager for her help and left to find this new accommodation.

The 'Sea Breeze' swinging house sign came into view as we walked down Nelson Road, and on arriving outside we could see immediately that it looked a very nice place. Painted white and blue with pot plants either side of the front door, snow white net curtains up to the windows and a 'No Vacancies' sign in one of the lower windows. On ringing the bell, a lady opened the door and we took this to be Mrs Cassington, a middle-aged lady, probably mid-thirties but very attractive, tall with long black hair, smartly dressed with a nice figure too. She immediately invited us in, saying, 'You must be the two lads that have had quite a nasty experience.'

'Yes,' I said, as we both stood there drooling at this very attractive landlady.

Harry gave her our names and a step-by-step rundown of events, since we arrived yesterday here in Yarmouth.

'Yes,' said Mrs Cassington, 'I do understand the situation.' And as we walked inside, she commented further, 'It's places like that that gives all guest houses a bad name.'

At that Mrs Cassington said, 'Right, given the circumstances, I will take you up and show you the only room I've got, that you can have. It's an extension on the side of the house that I use personally and I don't usually let it out, but if you think it's ok, that's fine with me.'

We followed Mrs Cassington up a flight of stairs to the first floor and then along the landing to a door at the very end. She opened the door and we all walked in. We saw two single beds, one on the left wall and another on the right, neatly made up with colourful bedspreads and, to my delight, two pillows on each. There was a wardrobe on the wall behind the door and a chest of draws the other side. We followed Mrs Cassington to the far end of the bedroom, which was fully carpeted, and she pointed out a metal spiral staircase at this end which, she said, led down to the bathroom. At this she continued to walk down this spiral staircase with Harry in tow; I stayed behind, looking round the bedroom, thinking that this was paradise compared with the other place.

Harry and Mrs Cassington walked straight into this bathroom at the bottom of the stairs, as there was no door in between. In fact the only door in the bathroom, apparently led into another of Mrs Cassington's own rooms. She told Harry that she had this extension built for her to live in during the summer when the house was fully occupied. She had her own sitting room and bedroom but would have to use this bathroom as well, but not to worry about that because she would have to be up very early in the mornings to start breakfast duties and would be out of our way before we got up. The bathroom was nicely decorated with a huge bath, fancy sink and a toilet with a polished wooden seat.

Both returned up the spiral staircase and Harry, all smiles, looked at me, already nodding his head in approval.

'It's not one of my best rooms,' said Mrs Cassington. 'I use it occasionally when my relatives want to visit, but if you think it's ok, I will do it at a special price of four pounds and ten shillings for the rest of this week, including breakfast. I will leave you lads to have a chat and you can let me know if you want to take it when you come back down.'

After she left the room, Harry said, 'Alf, I don't know what you're thinking but this will do us. It's nice, bright and clean with our own bathroom, and this location is handy for getting down to the prom.'

'I agree, I think we have landed on our feet here and the lower price makes up a little for what we have lost at the other place, let's go down and say yes. We then have the job of getting our stuff out of the other place, hopefully unseen.'

After thanking Mrs Cassington, we left and arrived back at

Selbourne House; at least the van was parked right outside for a quick getaway, and it was fortunate that the big guy was not on the door so we sneaked in as quietly as we could, back up to the room. Grabbing our stuff, I said, 'It might be best if we take one suitcase down first before we do a runner with the other.'

'No,' said Harry. 'I'm not afraid. We are going down together and if "Old Mother Riley" is about, we'll give her what for.'

We arrived downstairs to find Mrs Riley, unfortunately, just coming out of the dining room. She looked at us and then the suitcases in our hands and said, 'Where do you think you're going?'

'We are leaving, we are not stopping here a moment longer,' I said.

'Then you owe me money,' she said.

Harry said, 'We owe you nothing. You've had all the money you are getting. This place is a den of iniquity and we have been advised by the authorities, who incidentally are aware of what's going on in here, to seek alternative accommodation.'

At this, 'The Oaf' appeared on the scene for some action and took a step forward. Even Eddie from the dairy, thinking about it, wouldn't want to mess with this fucker.

'And you can piss off,' said Harry, him taking a step backwards just in case a punch was on its way, 'or we're straight round the cop shop to report you and this place, tell them what's been happening here.'

At this Mrs Riley grabbed the oaf's arm and pulled him back, telling him to back off, adding, 'We don't need any trouble right now, let them leave.'

So with us still shaking, we left 'Old Mother Riley' and Selbourne House, gave a sigh of relief and happily drove off to our new digs.

Chapter 11

We parked the van outside the 'Sea Breeze' guest house and carried our things up to our room. Having sorted out who was sleeping where and who was having which drawers, we decided that this time we would unpack our cases completely.

Having freshened up in our own basement bathroom, we both put on fresh shirts in our quest to hit the promenade, going all out to find the talent.

We left our room, and this time we were able to lock it. When we got downstairs, Mrs Cassington came out of the lounge and held up a key, telling us that it was a key to the front door and that there were no rules on times, but asking us to be very quiet when we come in, respecting the other guests. This key she held out to Harry and placed it into the palm of his hand. Closing his hand with her two hands she said, 'Don't lose it.'

When we got outside, I said to Harry, 'Mrs Cassington is very friendly, which is nice.'

'Yes, she is. Giving me the key she squeezed my hand, but I think it's more a case of don't lose it or else.'

'I had noticed. In fact there's a certain mystique about her, don't you think?'

The promenade and beach was as busy as usual as we made our way down to the Britannia Pier. At one point, as we strutted along, we looked down on to the beach and saw the ever popular Punch and Judy booth, with all the children sat round out front, shouting with great gusto when the crocodile appeared and laughing loudly when Punch hits the policeman. As a kid I always found Punch a bit frightening. I think it was the nose.

Stretching out into the sea with its wooden walkway, the pier was also very busy with people enjoying the sunshine, some eating ice creams, some playing the slot machines in the penny arcades, and you could hear music coming from the children's amusement rides. We decided to walk the length of the pier. On reaching the end, fishermen were baiting their lines, then casting out to sea, as far as they could. Small boys dangled their crab lines over the sides. All in all, a great holiday atmosphere. Harry and I stood at the railings taking in the sea air and finally feeling that we were now on holiday, sun, sea and sand, but alas, still no girls we would want to mix with, and the girls we did see were a case of 'Don't like yours.'

'I think what we should do now is head further on down the prom,' said Harry, 'and go to the Pleasure Beach funfair, we are bound to see more girls there.'

This we did, and as we walked along you could see the Big Dipper roller coaster and hear the screams from the people on the ride. The two people sitting in the front of the first car, having overcome their fears presumably, had raised their arms in the air as the cars plunged down the other side before making that clack-clack-clacking sound as the cars engaged the cogs again to rise up the next incline and rattle down the next.

'Harry, we will have to go on that,' I said.

'And the bumper cars,' Harry replied.

On entering the fair, the whole place was full of colour and fun, light bulbs everywhere and music coming from all directions. We could see the waltzers ahead of us, spinning round with a mixture of screams and laughter coming our way.

'There's always girls on there, they love the waltzers. Let's take a look,' said Harry.

We watched the waltzers spinning freely round and up and down at the same time on the undulating track, all great fun. The waltzer riders, that is to say, the chaps who work on the ride, risk danger by giving the cars that extra fast spin. The girl's just love it. Standing on the gangway that surrounds the ride, we await our turn, watching the gaily coloured cars going round, generally with up to four people in them held in with a central bar. The riders targeted some girls already screaming, and made the car spin round with such force they were all over the place, with legs akimbo.

The ride slowed down and eventually stopped, the hand rail in the front of the car was raised and people got off. This was where everyone waiting, runs to get on. Harry and I made a dash for one of the cars and ended up having to sit next to a couple of girls that got there before us. Having paid, the ride started off and it wasn't long before we were all thrown to one side and then the other. The girl next to me screamed and we all gripped the hand rail to try to keep our place. It was great fun, and when the ride stopped, Harry asked one of the two girls what they were going on next. 'The ghost train,' came back the reply. 'It's up here if you want to tag along, it's a dark ride and full of horror.'

Thinking we might have clicked with these two girls, Harry and I duly followed. The ghost train had just stopped with people getting off, some looking a little pale whilst others were in hysterics. The two girls we had just met split up, one in one car and the other in the car behind. So Harry jumped in with one of the girls and me the other.

I was in the front train car and, turning to the girl by me, I said, 'It's best if we hold on to one another,' promptly putting my arm around her shoulder as we started off. Looking back, I saw Harry had done the same. As we started off a sign warned us to 'Keep arms and legs in and do not stand.' Then with menacing laughter from hidden speakers, we burst through the metal doors with a loud bang, disappearing from daylight into complete darkness and the unknown. We were subjected to sharp turns of direction, flashing lights, high-pitched screams, and as we passed through Dracula's den, a mummified figure suddenly shot up in front of us. Something brushed my forehead, feeling very much like walking into a spider's web, closely followed by a fine mist of water on my face. We descended into the bowels of gruesome ghosts and spooks of all kinds, dancing all around us making weird sounds. We then turned towards a figure in a cage, covered in blood, moaning and groaning. His outstretched hand beckoned to us for help. On my side further up front, I saw another hand appear in a shaft of light coming right towards me. Suddenly, without warning, I got a very hard slap across the face. Shit, that was for real, that was not mechanical, some fucker had just given me a right old slapping. I turned round to see that someone, disappearing into the darkness. A moment later the car suddenly picked up speed before crashing through the exit doors as the ride came to an end and we were back outside in the daylight.

I immediately turned to the girl and said, 'Someone in there has just given me a right old slap across the face.'

'Oh, that will be my boyfriend,' came back the reply, 'he works the ghost train. He must have seen you and me together and got a bit jealous.'

'A bit jealous, No shit,' I said as I jumped out. 'You could have warned me.'

Harry joined me, saying, 'Forget these two, we are wasting our time.'

'Too rights, mate, the girl I was with was taking the piss.'

As we walked away, I explained to Harry what had just taken place, much to his amusement.

Next up for us was the roller coaster ride, a huge wooden structure designed to look like a mountain, with the various train cars at different stages along the ride.

'Alf, there is a big queue for this one, you wait in it while I get us some drinks.'

'Sure. After this though, we need to get some food. My stomach is rumbling.'

'Just as well then, you won't bring much up if you're sick on the ride.'

It didn't take long before we were at the front of the queue and grabbing a seat on the next car to go, sitting just in front of the brakeman, who sits between the two cars, his job being to control the speed. Harry asked him how fast we would go. To which he replied, with a laugh, 'That all depends on me and the brakes, but with thirty riders it can be up to forty-five miles per hour.'

With the manual security lap bars locked in place we started off, moving along slowly at first, then after gripping the running chain gear underneath we were off with a clack-clack-clack, as it pulled the cars up the first steep rise. Reaching the top we descended down, gathering momentum, bunny hopping over the next stretch, all the time gathering speed in the process. Then another even higher rise before descending again, followed with some more twists and turns. We passed signs telling us to sit down at all times for our own safety, and the ride carried on with some large drops, one nicknamed the Head Chopper because the train car dived down just under part of the overhead support structure. Eventually, we arrived at the biggest incline, the chain lift hill. Again the running gear clicked back into place with the usual clack, clack, clack, as we get pulled up the hill to the top of this big one. The view was fantastic with views across the bay and with raised arms from the two girls sat in the front seats, we thundered down the other side, some 70 feet, in a crescendo of screams. Harry and I got off, feeling exhilarated but somewhat unsteady, both of us undecided as to whether we should queue up again for another go. But we thought the better of it, getting some food now was more important.

'We can always come back again another time, if we want to,' said Harry. 'So where shall we go to eat?'

'I think we should go back to that Lilly's café and eat there, where we went this morning. We can also thank the waitress for putting us in touch with the information advice centre.'

'Yes, that's ok with me; I like it in there. The food's good too and they've got a juke box.'

We arrived at Lilly's café and the waitress remembered us and said hello straight away. We quickly explained to her what had transpired and thanked her for her help.

'Take a seat, but not the one in the window,' said the waitress.

We sat down, again wondering what was so special about that seat in the window, but no matter. Having placed our order, we sat chatting, feeling quite happy with ourselves having escaped the clutches of Old Mother Riley. Harry got up and picked a record on the jukebox. We sat there listening to his selection, 'Runaway', recorded by Del Shannon, reminding us of our quick getaway from Selbourne House. After a while, Harry nudged me to take a look at someone who had just come in. This person walked straight away over to the table in the window. A man in his early thirties I would think, very smartly dressed in a mohair suit. At least I think it was mohair, it had that sheen to it and looked very expensive, as was his classy shirt with tie to match.

'Smart bloke,' Harry, said to me, as the man sat down at the table, the table in the window.

'Yes,' I replied, 'and important too I guess, hence the window seat. I bet he's worth a bob or two.'

'Well his suit probably costs more than I earn in a year.'

At that the waitress immediately went over and engaged in conversation with this man, and after chatting to him for a while she wrote down his coffee and cake order.

Our order came and we tucked into egg, beans and chips with gusto, swallowed down with a nice hot cup of sweet tea. The café was still quite packed, considering it was late in the day. Probably not all holidaymakers though, some locals as well. This was not surprising really, because the café served good food in nice clean surroundings and at reasonable prices.

The smartly dressed man sat in the window, having had his coffee and cake, acknowledged the waitress, smiled at us and left walking towards the theatre. We watched him as he crossed the road and walked into the theatre.

Thinking of what we might get up to for the rest of tonight, I said to Harry, 'It might be best, as we've had a full day, just to go to the local pub for a drink. You know, the one on the corner of the road where we are staying. Then tomorrow we can patrol the promenade and beach and, hopefully, get to chat up some girls. We might even bump into those girls we met when we first arrived.'

'Ah, Joan and her mates,' replied Harry. 'Can't get the one out of your mind, can you?'

'They were all ok, but I quite fancied two of them.'

'Let me guess, I bet it was that Joan, and the other one being Sandra.'

'Spot on,' I replied and at that we got up, gave our thanks to the waitress and left the café.

So we had a couple of brown and milds in the Red Lion pub and got back to the guest house around ten. Lights were still on but we tried to be quiet going up to our room, and it wasn't long before Harry and I had crashed out in our new surroundings.

Chapter 12

As I rolled over, the early-morning light filtered through a gap in the curtains. I'd had a good night's sleep and saw that Harry was already awake, sitting on the side of his bed.

'You're up early,' I said, sitting up. 'What time is it?'

'Morning. Actually it's nearly 7am. I'm going to take a bath and start the day with a walk to get a newspaper before breakfast.'

'Rather you than me. I'll leave it for another half hour and then make a start.' At that I buried myself under the sheet, closed my eyes and drifted off to sleep again, leaving Harry to carry on with his ablutions.

Harry grabbed his towel and toilet bag, and with just his pyjama bottoms on, set off down the spiral staircase to have his bath. On reaching the bottom he turned into the bathroom to find Mrs Cassington, our landlady, standing there semi naked with her back towards him as she looked into the bathroom mirror. With only a little pink towel round her middle, Harry could see the outline of her breasts in the steamed up mirror.

'Oh! Sorry,' said Harry quickly, without taking his eyes off the mirror. 'I thought you would be done by this time in the morning.'

'Normally I would have been,' she said, still looking in the mirror, 'but I got delayed with a phone call, more guests wanting to stay here.'

At that, Mrs Cassington twisted and turned round in front of the mirror to face Harry, giving him a front row view of her breasts, saying, 'It's ok, I have finished now. You can come in and I will leave you to it.'

As she spoke, Harry just stared at her breasts, thinking how beautifully formed they were and how sexy she looked with her long wet hair draped over her shoulders.

Mrs Cassington pushed open the door to her apartment; half turned round, smiled at Harry and went inside, closing the door behind her. Harry, still in shock, placed his towel down on a stool and could only stand there for a moment, looking at himself in the mirror, thinking how beautifully mature Mrs Cassington was and certainly a woman without any inhibitions.

He quickly bathed and had a shave and was about to leave and return back up to the bedroom when Mrs Cassington's door opened. Still in a state of undress, except for a loose-fitting silk dressing gown, she quietly said, 'Harry could you pop in and sort out my table lamp, I think it may have a bulb gone or something. That's if you've finished bathing.'

As though in some sort of automatic mode, and desperately trying to be unaffected by the bathroom occurrence, Harry replied, 'I'm not an electrician, but I will have a look. It may be just a loose connection.'

Harry followed Mrs Cassington back into her bedroom. Mrs Cassington turned and closed the door behind them, then pointed to the faulty lamp on the dresser. On investigation, Harry found the bulb in the lamp did not appear to be loose. So he checked that the plug was fully in and then tried the switch. The bulb, as if by magic, did in fact light up. A little puzzled, Harry turned round, saying that the lamp appeared to be ok and that she was probably right, just a loose connection.

Mrs Cassington, however, was by now standing at the end of her bed, and in a soft voice said, 'Come over here, Harry.' At that she dropped her dressing gown down to the floor.

Harry, who, again, could only focus on her breasts, walked over very unsure and wondering what was next to come. Mrs Cassington unwrapped the towel around her waist, slowly letting that also drop to the floor and lay back on the bed, shuffling up to place her head on the pillow, posing like a model on a film set, one arm behind her head, legs crossed with one slightly raised. She curled her finger and beckoned Harry to join her.

Harry, whose heart by now was racing nineteen to the dozen, felt nervous and no longer sure as to what was happening. He stood with eyes wide open, looking down at her as she lay there, all woman and beautiful. Her body looking silky smooth, her skin unblemished and standing out against the blue and white bed spread. She was certainly fit all right, a rather mature lady, yes, but toned and everything in the right places, and now that his brain was in gear, he realised that an invitation to have sex was about to take place.

'I lost my husband some time ago. I loved him, I really did, but I get lonely and I still have needs. Do you know what I mean, Harry?' she asked.

All that Harry could do was slightly nod his head, as he stood there transfixed.

Mrs Cassington uncrossed her legs, revealing her dark and neat looking pubic hair, trimmed to perfection. Harry, feeling rather weak at the knees by now and realising what she meant, went into auto-pilot and pulled the cord on his pyjama waistband, dropping his bottoms to the floor, revealing his unintended excitement. Mrs Cassington raised her knees, and then lowered them to the side. Harry, now so helplessly in the control of Mrs Cassington, knelt on the bed. He slowly lowered himself down on to her and whilst looking into her eyes, he whispered, 'This is just between you and me, Mrs Cassington, we must treat it as being just a dream.'

'Sweet dreams then,' she replied.

As he began to push inside her, she controlled her vaginal muscles accordingly and both gave it everything. She's a lady of few words, Harry thought, and requires no foreplay.

A few minutes later Harry re-emerged back into the bathroom, quietly shutting the door behind him, leaving Mrs Cassington to get dressed. He just stared at himself in the mirror for a moment, not really believing what had just taken place. How would he ever beat that for an impromptu shag? He quickly gathered up his towel and toilet bag and made his way up the staircase, finding me with my towel in hand, coming down.

'I couldn't wait any longer mate,' I said. 'You've been absolutely ages in the bath, I hope you haven't used up all the hot water.'

'Sorry, mate, I fell asleep in the bath,' he said, as he continued up to the bedroom.

'Well you won't have time before breakfast to go for a walk now,' I shouted.

'No worries, I don't feel up to taking a walk now anyway.'

I spent a lot less time in the bathroom than Harry did, and returned back up to the bedroom, finding Harry tidying up his bed clothes.

The breakfast gong in the hall could be heard, indicating

that breakfast was now being served, and having decided to put on our new clothes and show off today, we both quickly got dressed in our new jackets and trousers we bought from Zissman's, plus our new white moccasins. Maybe being dressed like this would just get us noticed, as we paraded ourselves down the promenade on the lookout for girls.

We went downstairs into the hall, passing an old highly polished grandfather clock, which had begun to chime on the hour of eight as we entered the dining room. It was a hive of activity, with other guests already having breakfast, some reading their morning papers and others engrossed in looking at maps, presumably organising their day's activities. The guests looked up as we walked in to sit down at the only vacant table. A door swung open and a woman came out, says good morning to Harry and me and after giving us the breakfast menu, saying she would be back in a moment to take our order.

Harry said, 'That approach is certainly far different from the last place,' and began looking at the breakfast menu. The woman returned a few minutes later to take our order, asking if we were straight into having a cooked breakfast or would we like cereals first.

'I'm going to have the usual full breakfast with toast,' said Harry to the waitress, adding, 'Could you please ask the kitchen not to make the egg too runny?'

'Flipped, is what you mean,' said the waitress.

'Flipped,' replied Harry, puzzled.

'Your egg turned over,' I quietly said to Harry.

'Oh right, yes flipped thanks.'

'I would like the same as well please,' I replied.

'Would you like tea, or we've got Camp coffee?'

We answered and the waitress left, with Harry having buried his head in his napkin because one of the guests, a woman, continually looked over at us. Smiling and nodding, this woman eventually said good morning and offered to tell us the weather forecast for the day. Why does everyone talk about the weather as an opener? She followed it up by asking, 'Are you both with one of the theatres in the town, performing there perhaps?' Harry looked at me, smiled and with a grin on his face turned round to answer the woman, and not wishing to disappoint said, 'We are involved but not front of house.'

I leaned over to Harry and whispered, 'Where on earth did that come from, what's front of house?'

'Shhh, I read about it in a magazine. It means you work in the background, not on the stage as a performer.'

'Oh! I see, like a stand in, in case something goes wrong.'

'Not exactly,' said Harry, shaking his head.

Harry turned back to the woman, asking 'Why did you ask that question?'

'Oh it's because of your clothes, both of you being dressed the same that is. We have stayed here at the Sea Breeze before and met many theatre folk who also stay here when appearing in shows at the theatres; the Sea Breeze seems popular with the artists.'

Harry smiled back at her, straightened his knife and fork on the table, awaiting his breakfast, and we both had a titter to ourselves.

Fortunately right on cue, not having to answer any more questions, our breakfasts were put before us, nicely presented, and we both tucked in.

Harry said, half munching on his toast, 'This is a good breakfast.'

'It is,' I replied. 'But why is it that you have got two eggs and I've only got one?'

'It must be a mistake, mate, just a mistake.' Harry thought, I hope I'm not being favoured here, for services rendered. With breakfast over we decided to get going and head down to the prom for some action.

Upon checking that the van was still ok, we started off; the sun was just starting to deliver some heat. Harry reminded me that we must buy some sun cream and apply it before it got too hot, so we decided to find the local chemist first before hitting the sea front. That reminded me also that I needed to buy some Durex, and I mentioned this to Harry.

'You mean that you have come on holiday to meet girls, have sex, to get your initiation badge, and you've come away without any condoms,' said Harry.

'Well I did mean to get some, but I never had the time before we came away. The problem is though, it's nearly always a woman that comes to serve you.'

'You had the time, mate, what you really mean is that you were just too embarrassed to ask for them. Well, you will have to get some Durex, or go bareback riding and risk it.'

'What do you mean by that?' I said

Harry laughs and continues with, 'You know, apply the rhythm and withdraw method, and you will have to be in time with the beat or you will be in trouble, or should I say the girl will be.'

We found a chemist just round the corner, an old fashioned one with lots of funny shaped bottles in the window on wooden shelves. Going in we saw lots of wooden draws too, with labels on, and took in that kind of smell you always get in these sorts of places, like somebody's mixed a something kind of smell, but you don't know what it is.

A male assistant behind the counter, wearing a white coat, was using scales to weigh out some sort of powder for a customer.

I turned to Harry saying, 'Now if he serves me I'll be happy to ask him for a packet of three and buy the sun cream at the same time.'

'Fine, I will leave you to it then and wait outside in the sunshine.'

Harry disappeared outside at the same time the assistant in the white coat had finished serving his customer. I was just going to ask the assistant what I wanted, when he promptly walked away into the back, upon which a young pretty female assistant approached, all smiles, and asked if could she could help me. Feeling embarrassed, I paused for a moment, and then stuttered out that I needed protection.

'What sort of protection would that be?' she replied, still smiling.

Not wishing to be embarrassed further I said, 'Face cream, yes face cream, it's going to be a hot one today.' To this she reached for a jar of cream placed it on the counter, saying 'This is a good one, I use this myself,' and with that same smile she added, 'If you need any greater protection you will have to come back.' She knew, I'm sure, what I really wanted to buy. My face must have been crimson red, and having paid I opened the door and left.

Harry said, 'Did you get what you wanted.'

'Yes,' I replied. 'I'm ready for action.' Thinking to myself, I can't tell him I had bottled out. I will pop back later and get the condoms when the man assistant is in there serving.

Chapter 13

The promenade was already busy with people queuing at the kiosks, buying their seaside souvenirs and sticks of rock. As we walked along at a relatively slow pace, continuing to be on the lookout for girls, we noticed people staring at us as they passed by.

'That woman in the digs was right,' said Harry. 'You and I being dressed the same; people do think that we are in one of the theatre shows.'

'Yes well, please don't get into conversation with anybody, if they ask.'

'I can't wait to go the theatre and see the Big Star Show.'

We patrolled the promenade all morning, milking the looks that we were attracting. I was hoping we would bump into Joan and the girls. Unfortunately we didn't, and in fact we were short on attracting any girls. Then coming towards us was the couple we met the other night at Paddy's Bar, Mary and Bert.

'Hi, you two. How are you getting on?' said Bert. Mary stood there, clutching her handbag as usual.

'Well,' I said, 'we are ok now,' and spent the next ten minutes giving Mary and Bert a quick rundown about the accommodation problem that we first had.

'Selbourne House is well known for its goings on,' piped in

Mary. 'As I said to you the other night we've been coming here for years. You poor things, had I known that's where you two were staying, I would have warned you. In fact, Bert found out what that place was really like when he made some enquiries years ago. Bert was a trilby man before he retired and was able to get information on all sorts of people and places.'

'Trilby man,' I said. 'What's a trilby man? I've not heard that one before.'

'He was a detective in the police force before retiring, and they always wore trilby hats,' said Mary. 'They were known as the trilby boys.'

'Yes,' said Bert, 'after thirty-five years of lifting collars, I thought it was time to pack it in.'

Harry said, 'It seems to me that everybody and their grannies knew about Selbourne House except us two. Anyway we are sorted out now, especially where we are.'

'That's right, the digs we have now are great, our landlady is very nice and has been very accommodating, isn't that right, Harry?'

'Yes, extremely accommodating.'

'The landlady is a Mrs Cassington,' I said. 'She has done her best. Put us up in one of her own bedrooms and bent over backwards, you might say.'

Bert invited us to join them that night at Paddy's place, have a few drinks and no doubt all have a few laughs. We said that hopefully we would see them this evening, said goodbye and continued our walk down the promenade, stopping every so often at the railings, chatting and looking down on to the beach at people having fun.

Harry said, 'It's now coming up to lunch time. Shall we get

something to eat? Because I'm definitely in need of food again.'

'We've only just had breakfast.'

'Alf, that was four hours ago, I need to eat.'

'You're trying to keep your strength up, all you think about is food. Well that and girls of course.'

'You could say that we need to have the stamina, for when we do have a couple of girls in tow.'

So, not wishing to walk around eating fish and chips, we both decided we would go back again to Lilly's, after all, it was good food, they played music and they knew us there now. Plus they served the kind of food we like to eat. We were finding our way round the town quite well now and crossed the road by the Windmill Theatre to the café.

On entering Lilly's café, Harry gave me a nudge and pointed out that the well-dressed man was in again, sat at the table in the widow with a cup in his hand whilst reading a newspaper. He had a different colour suit on this time, still looking expensive and extremely smart. There was no doubt he goes to a very classy tailor, probably Saville Row in London.

As we walked towards a table near to this guy, he turned, looked up, and acknowledges us with a nod of the head, but this time eyeing us up and down at the same time, taking more notice it would seem in the way we were dressed. We sat down at a table and started to look at the day's menu, whilst listening to the sound of an Elvis Presley record being played on the juke box. As we were deciding what to have to eat, this well-dressed guy left his seat in the window and came over to our table,

'Hello lads, do you mind if I join you?'

I looked up at the man and then across at Harry, quickly wondering why this man would want to join us two.

'Sure, sit yourself down,' said Harry.

The man pulls out a chair, sits down saying. 'Couldn't help noticing you lads when you walked in. Are you two appearing on the pier show?'

Harry smiled and looked at me. I was thinking, whatever you say, Harry, don't tell him we are in a show for Christ's sake.

'Sorry, but we're not some sort of double act, appearing in a show. I know the way we're dressed suggests that, but we are not in showbiz at all. We just like to dress the same; Alfie and I are actually here on holiday for the week.'

'Well you sure do look the part. Please allow me to introduce myself, I'm Larry Parnes, personal manager to a number of stars, some of which are appearing here in Yarmouth on the "Big Star Show" at the Windmill just over the road.'

At that his hand was offered and we shook it in turn. I noticed the cuff links he was wearing and the expensive looking watch, and with both our mouths wide open, he continued with, 'Perhaps you would like to see the show whilst you are here?' At that he reached into his inside pocket, showing the blue silk lining to his jacket, and brought out two theatre tickets and placed them on the table in front of us.

'Have these with my compliments, lads,' he said, 'I'm sure you will enjoy it.'

Turning to Harry, I jumped straight in with, 'That's really nice of you, Harry and I would love to see the show, wouldn't we?'

'Absolutely,' came back an immediate reply, and Harry picked up the tickets to look at them.

Larry Parnes reached over and pointed out that the date and time was on the tickets and they were for the second house.

'We wanted to see one of the shows,' I said, 'so this is great.

We'll both really look forward to going, Mr Parnes.'

'Please, call me Larry.' He then got up to return to his table, and soon after drank his coffee and left the café, leaving Harry and I sat at our table feeling chuffed and still somewhat open mouthed. Our usual waitress then came over to take our order.

'You had a nice chat with Mr Parnes then, boys?' she said. 'He's such a nice guy, comes in here every day. Very generous as well.'

Harry said, 'That's right, we've been given tickets for the show over the road, saves us money not having to buy them. Apparently he is the manager for some of the stars appearing on the show.'

'That's right,' continued the waitress. 'He is the manager of Billy Fury, Tommy Steel, Marty Wilde and one or two others. Billy Fury and Marty are appearing here at the Windmill for the whole of the summer season.' We ordered our meal and excitedly chatted about our encounter with Mr Parnes, or should I say Larry.

Upon leaving the café we walked over to the theatre, a big building, with twin towers either side with windmill sails slap bang in the centre of the building. Below the sails was a big poster sign depicting the faces of the main stars of the show, Billy Fury's being the main one. We also noticed that the price of a ticket for the second house was eight shillings and sixpence.

'We have saved ourselves nearly a pound, thanks to "Larry". I'm pleased with that,' said Harry. 'When you think about it, if Selbourne House had not been the dump it was and us having to go out for breakfast, we may not have found this café and had our chance meeting with Mr Parnes.'

We did a little window shopping as we made our way back

to our digs, both thinking that before the holiday was over we might just buy a gift to take back home to the girls. After getting back to the Sea Breeze, we rested on our beds and chatted for a while, before getting ready for the evening. I was looking forward to an evening walk along the prom and then a drink down at Paddy's Bar.

Having changed our clothes into something more comfortable for the evening, we were about to leave the room when there was a knock on the bedroom door.

'Come in,' said Harry and the door opened. In the doorway stood Mrs Cassington looking all done up, nice like, as if she too was just about to go out for the evening. Tailored black slacks, pink floral top, high heels, and her hair fixed up in a bun, plus bright red lipstick.

'Oh! Hi,' I said. 'Please, do come in.'

'No I won't come in, I only wondered if you had settled in and if there was anything you needed?'

'Well thank you, Mrs Cassington,' I replied, 'everything is just great; we are very comfortable, thanks to you.'

Mrs Cassington eyeballed Harry, saying, 'Is there anything that you might need later?'

'No, we have everything for now.' After pausing for a moment Harry added, 'I must say you're looking very nice this evening, are you going out somewhere special?'

'No I'm not going out; I don't always look my best during the day, especially in the mornings.' At that point, looking directly at Harry, she continued with, 'So I dress up in the evening, relax with a drink. It makes me feel good.'

Harry knew that she had paid us a visit just to show herself off. To see her in a different light, you might say, morning to evening. At that Mrs Cassington smiled and left.

'That was good of her to check on us,' I said.

We left the digs and made our way down to the seafront, hoping that this time, as we sauntered along the promenade making our way down to Paddy's Bar, we might meet some girls. Harry said it was strange that we hadn't bumped into the four girls we met on our first day here.

'Yes, it is a bit strange; we could try the beach tomorrow if you like, they may be sun worshipers and early to bed.'

'I wouldn't mind going early to bed with that Sandra.'

'I wouldn't mind seeing Joan in her bathing costume.'

'Is that the one you fancy then?' said Harry.

'I just want to get some experience, but yes I think she's really nice. But it could be with any one of them. I'm more frustrated than a frustrated person; you must be feeling the same, Harry.'

'Well yes, I could do with dipping my wick; I haven't had sex for a while, not since Dianne anyway.'

As we walked along, the sea was looking very calm. People were still swimming and larking about in the sea. The donkeys had been gathered up, tethered one behind the other in a line having done their bit for the day and now walking towards the slope, going back to their stables for the night. Sandcastles that the kids had built littered the shoreline, left abandoned to the incoming tide that would eventually take them over, returning them to a flat state for the sand to be used all over again on another day.

The Punch and Judy man had all his puppets hanging up on the outside of his little blue and white stripped theatre as he packed up his things for the day, having entertained untold kids and their parents alike. You could just hear screams in the distance from people as they descended the big drop on the roller coaster at the Pleasure Beach. Across the road, the so-called Golden Mile, you could hear the caller in one of the many bingo games calling out the numbers, two little ducks number two, number nine the Brighton Line, however, that's not something we would be interested in doing, that's for old folks.

Harry fancied some cockles again, so we stopped at the stall and had a dish each.

There's something about having a taste of the sea as you look and admire it. We both stood, taking in all the magic of the seaside on this warm summer's night, with just a slight sea breeze filling our nostrils before we carried on down the promenade.

Continuing down the prom, Harry said to me, 'Look who's walking towards us; it's that Joan and her friends.'

We moved over a little to make sure that that we would bump into them.

'Wow girls,' Harry said, as we all stopped, 'you all look great.'

The girls looked as pretty as a picture; they all had summer minidresses on, in nice bright colours, wide belts pulled in tight at the waist, showing off their figures, their hair done up nicely and all carrying handbags. I must say Joan looked very womanly, sexy and fresh. I think she was probably the oldest out of the four.

'Hello,' said one of the girls, 'fancy meeting you two again.'

'It's good to see you,' replied Harry. 'What are you up to, all dressed up and that?'

Joan said, 'We are off to the Windmill Theatre; we are going to see Billy Fury and Marty Wilde on the Big Star Show.'

'Well it just so happens,' I said, 'Harry and I are going

tomorrow night; and you'll never guess where we got our tickets from.'

'Go on then, tell us, we are all ears,' said one of the girls.

I carried on, saying, 'We were in a café and got talking to a guy who turned out to be the manager of Billy Fury and other stars appearing on the show. He has given us complimentary tickets to see the show, so we are going tomorrow night.'

'That's amazing,' said Joan. 'How lucky are you.'

Ruby, one of the girls, said, 'Will you get to meet the stars as well? I've got a right crush on Billy Fury.'

Joan chipped in with, 'I prefer Marty Wilde, he's my kind of man.'

'I don't know if we will get to see them personally,' said Harry. 'We will have to wait and see.'

Joan said they needed to get a move on, as they didn't want to miss the start of the show. As they were leaving, Harry asked the girls what they were doing tomorrow.

Sandra replied, saying that they were hoping to have a day on the beach tomorrow, take their costumes and, if the weather was nice, go for a swim in the sea. I replied that we may do the same, so we might just see them around.

'Fine,' said Joan. 'It will be nice to see you, but we must go now, bye.'

At that, they left for the theatre and we continued on down to Paddy's Bar, with me still having an image of Joan in her bathing costume. Crossing the road to Paddy's Bar we could see Mary and Bert already sipping away with their drinks. They saw us approaching and waved and pointed out that they had kept some seats for us.

'What a lovely evening,' said Mary, as we both sat down.

'Yes it is, and thanks for saving the seats for us.'

Harry got up straight away and went inside to get the drinks, and I asked Mary where they were staying in Yarmouth.

'Tide's Reach is where we stay, have done so for years. We always have, bed with breakfast and evening dinner. It's home from home and it suits us just fine.'

'That's nice,' I said. 'We are only bed and breakfast, but we have found a nice café where the food is really good. In fact, when Harry and I were in there today we met a man who is the manager of Billy Fury, one of the singers appearing at the Windmill Theatre and he's given us tickets to see the show.'

'How nice is that,' said Mary.

Harry came back with the drinks and Bert kicked off with a joke as usual, much to Mary's disgust.

'Two fellas, one named Arthur and the other named Cyril, and they have both got something wrong with them. They've heard about this convent that cures people, so along they go.

Arthur knocks on the door of the convent.

A nun opens the door and says, "Yes, my son?"

Arthur says, "I've had to use these crutches all my life and I want to get rid of them."

She says, "Come on in, my son," and she takes him in to a room full of nuns and says, "Stand behind this curtain and we will all pray for you."

Then Cyril knocks on the door of the convent.

The nun opens the door and says, "Yes, my son?"

Cyril says, "I've had a st … st … st … stutter all my life and I'd like to get rid of it."

She says, "Come on in, my son," and the nun takes him into the room full of nuns and says, "Stand behind the curtain and we will all pray for you."

After ten minutes of praying the nun shouts, "Arthur, Arthur, throw out your crutches."

And sure enough, a pair of crutches come flying out from behind the curtain.

Then the nun shouts, "Cyril, Cyril speak to me."

And Cyril says, "Ar ... Ar ... Ar ... Arthur's fallen over'"

I nearly choked on my drink with that one. We all fell about laughing, including those sitting around us.

Harry said, 'Bert you are quite the entertainer. I don't know how you remember them, if someone tells me a joke, you can bet I've forgotten it five minutes later.'

From that point onwards we had various people, who were sat on the terrace drinking and enjoying the fun, jumping in with their own jokes as well. The warm evening continued, with us all drinking and chatting. The holiday atmosphere was in full swing, combined with the smell of the sea wafting over from the beach adding to the moment. People were still parading up and down the prom but Harry and I decided to call it a night. We said our goodbyes to everyone and made our way back to our digs for hopefully another good night's sleep and to enjoy another a good day tomorrow.

It wasn't long before we arrived back and got into our room, with both of us crashing out as soon as our heads touched the pillows; it had to be the sea air, possibly the two pillows, or could it have been the drink?

Chapter 14

I could tell it was starting to get light despite my eyes still being closed, my head half buried under the sheets because of the early-morning cries from the seagulls. Whilst I hate them for the scavengers that they are, they do happen to be a good alarm clock. I decided to lie in for a while longer, pulling the sheet up even higher; I was feeling well rested and dreaming of meeting up with Joan and her mates. I wondered if Harry was right when he said he thought Joan fancied me. The problem, for me, is being rejected if you make a play.

In between the cry of the seagulls, I started to hear more unfamiliar noises, sniffing, the odd cough, whispering and shuffling sounds. It didn't sound like Harry getting up, so I slowly pulled the sheet down, just enough to see what was happening. With eyes only half open I made out a bloke standing beside my bed. Dressing gown on, reading a book, a towel over his shoulder and what looked like a toilet bag under his arm. This can't be real, I thought, pulling the sheet back over my head, I must still be dreaming, tell me I'm dreaming. Only to pull the sheet back down again and this time seeing a second person standing behind him, this being a woman also in a dressing gown, with a towel in her hand.

She smiled at me and then said, 'Good morning, I think it's

going to be a nice day.'

I sat up in bed, mouth wide open on seeing these two people standing in between our two beds and amazingly, and rather politely for me, given the shock of it, I simply asked, 'Never mind the weather forecast, what the hell is going on here? How did you two get in?'

The man looking down at me said he was waiting to use the bathroom but his daughter was in there at the moment and apologised to me for the delay. 'Oh, and by the way,' he said, 'I'm George, and this is my wife Carol. But don't worry, we will both go in the bathroom together, to speed things up.'

'Well thanks for the introductions, mate, but this is our bedroom and the bathroom down the stairs is ours. Well, that is to say, ours and Mrs Cassington's.'

By now Harry had stirred and rolled over to see what was going on. Startled, he too sat up quickly and looking across at me said, 'What the fuck is going on, and who the fuck are these people?'

Before I could answer, the man, realising the situation was about to get a bit heated, quickly explained about a problem with a water leak in their bathroom upstairs and that the floor was now running with water. 'We told Mrs Cassington about it first thing this morning and she said we would have to use this one downstairs until it was fixed, which she said would be sometime today. She has turned off the water for the moment and is cleaning our bathroom floor as we speak.'

Harry, embarrassed by his outburst and trying to be a bit more polite said, 'Thanks for the update on the cleaning, mate, but how the hell did you get in to our room?'

'The door was unlocked and we thought, as you were both

asleep, we could sneak in and be out in next to no time, but Rose, our daughter, has been in there far too long, typical today of the younger generation.'

'I take that as meaning younger than us,' I said, sitting up in bed.

Footsteps could be heard, breaking up the conversation, as their daughter came up the spiral staircase and back into our room. Dressed in only her underwear, this vision from heaven, probably aged about sixteen or seventeen, stood in front of us in the tightest of knickers, showing off her cracking figure.

The man turned to us, saying, 'This is our daughter, Rose.'

Well the sight of this girl standing there left Harry and I, still sitting up in bed, totally gobsmacked. The fact we had trespassers didn't seem to matter anymore. With our mouths still wide open, her parents now descended the stairs to our bathroom, saying that they wouldn't be long. The daughter, Rose, headed towards the door, stopped, turned round and without any inhibitions for being sparsely clad, stood there apologising for having to use the lower bathroom.

Harry was still transfixed, his eyes never moved above her waist. Rose, a platinum-blonde-headed girl, fabulous looking with beautiful white teeth, had a pink bra on, holstering undoubtedly small but beautifully formed breasts. Her bra matched her knickers, which had a touch of white lace round the edges. I could have had an orgasm just looking at her, but trying to compose myself I said, 'What's your name again?'

'Rose,' she said. 'I did knock gently before I entered your bedroom, but you two were both fast asleep. So I crept very quietly through and down the stairs so as not to wake you boys up.'

Harry and I, having calmed down completely, were now

happy to just stare at this vision from heaven. Both possibly wondering which one of us was going to take this beautiful maiden into our arms with a passion above all passions.

Without warning Rose then asked, 'Are you two boys sexually experienced?'

Well, our jaws dropped immediately again. Stunned, I looked at Harry, then at Rose and then back at Harry, both of us taken back with a question like that, from such an innocent looking girl. So, not only a vision from heaven, but talks dirty as well. Harry without doubt would mention his various conquests, as for myself, I was about to lie profusely. Or could it be that a threesome may be on the cards? Surely not here at the respectable Sea Breeze, but maybe she's not the angel she looks.

But before our mouths had time to close and answer Rose's question, she followed up by hitting us both between the eyes with, 'In six months' time I will be sixteen and old enough then for sex. I've heard from other girls that it's an experience that I must try.'

At that, Rose turned round to leave and go back to her own bedroom. Our eyes were transfixed as we followed Rose's bottom all the way to the door. On leaving, you'd think we had x-ray eyes as we both still continued staring at a closed door.

'Talk about falling back to earth with a bump,' Harry said, lying back down. 'Was she just teasing us? Either way I don't think somehow we'll be finding out on this holiday. Besides, I don't fancy going to jail.'

Before we had time to draw breath, there was a knock on the door and in walked Mrs Cassington, saying she was sorry about all the activity. Mrs Cassington was still in her dressing gown, bright red with white flowers and low cut. She was showing most of her breasts and apologising to us for the others having to use the bathroom, continuing by saying that a plumber was on his way to fix the leak and that she had mopped up the water and it was now drying out.

'Did you give them a key to get in?' Harry asked.

'No, I didn't,' said Mrs Cassington. 'I told them to knock on your door and ask if they could use the bathroom, but only after you two had got up ready for the day. Obviously you were both in deep slumber and they must have decided to go ahead anyway, having found the door unlocked.'

I said, 'Well, we had quite a few drinks last night, but a good night mind you, good company and lots of laughs.'

Mrs Cassington said, pointing to Harry with a wry smile on her face, 'That means you left the door unlocked last night, you naughty boy, so it's your fault really. So you can hardly complain about the Jones family. Anyway they are a charming family with a lovely daughter. I will bring you both a cup of tea in bed tomorrow morning, as a treat.' At that, Mrs Cassington left, closing the door.

Harry looked at me and said, 'She is certainly right about Rose. I thought for a moment when Rose asked if we were into sex that one of us was about to get our end away.'

I laughed and said, 'Or both of us. Anyway I think she's the sort that would go crying to mommy if we gave her one.'

'I wouldn't be too sure of that. Anyway, we need to be getting ready for a day on the beach, we're supposed to be meeting up with Joan and her mates.'

At that the Mr and Mrs Jones came up from the bathroom, apologising again, and said they had left the bathroom all tidy and hoped we would have a nice day.

With both of us having finally bathed and with nice clean T-shirts on, we went down to breakfast. The dining room was quite full and quiet, but for the radio playing 'Good luck charm' by Elvis. The Jones family were tucking into their breakfasts. Rose looked across as we sat down, looking fab in a pair of white shorts and a tank top in blue. If only she was six months older, I kept thinking, whilst eating my breakfast, she's going to be someone's conquest for the future and there's me still trying hard to lose my virginity on this holiday, which I'm not finding easy to do.

I leaned over and whispered to Harry, 'Looking at that girl is really pissing me off.'

'Alf, you need to slow your pecker down. If we are going to get a shag at all, our best bet is to get down to the prom and find Joan and the girls, because it's going to be with one of them. And another thing, Alf, when we are on the way down to the beach, you need to call in at the chemist and get yourself some condoms; I know you didn't get any the last time. Remember, Scouts motto, "Be Prepared".'

'Your right, of course, the problem was a girl came to serve me. However, I do need to be ready for action, if only for when we return home. I'm sure, as I've said before, I think Moira knows what to do and I don't want to be fumbling about like some school kid.'

We finished breakfast, grabbed our towels and swimming trunks and set off for a day on the beach. On the way we arrived at the chemist shop and went in, hoping to find the man serving this time to save any embarrassment on my part. A man did come out from the back room and said, 'Are you being served?'

'No we aren't,' Harry said. 'My mate here wants to buy something.'

'Oh right, I'm just dispensing some medication in the back room,' said the man. 'I will get my assistant to help you.'

I could have guessed who would come to serve me; it just had to be the girl, the same girl assistant who served me before.

'Hello,' she said, with a twinkle in her eye. 'Do you need more protection?'

She knew exactly what I had come in for previously, and it wasn't the sun cream I bought. I stood there in a trance, couldn't speak, and after my pregnant pause, Harry jumped in with, 'He's hoping for a shag, love, before our holiday is over, and needs a couple of condoms, one for safety, two if his luck is still running.' Harry then turned round saying, 'There you are, sorted, and I'll see you outside.'

Now it wasn't just my embarrassment, because the assistant by now was also bright red in the face as she bent down for the Durex, which they kept under the counter. Why do chemists always keep contraceptives, or as Harry refers to them, jumping socks, under the counter?

The assistant, having composed herself, duly placed them on the counter and I quickly paid and apologised to her for Harry's comments.

'No problem,' she said. 'Lots of boys are lacking in the use of adjectives.'

On my way out of the shop, the assistant very quietly said, 'Thanks, do come again.'

I thought if I come at all it will be a miracle! I turned round and smiled, thanked her and closed the door behind me.

'You put me on the spot in there, you bastard.'

'Well, what did you want to do, risk getting a girl up the duff? Anyway it's sorted now, let's hit the prom.'

Chapter 15

Having had a go at Harry, I put the condoms away securely. We made our way down to the seafront and started to walk the promenade, on the lookout for Joan and the girls. Another beautiful morning with a nice gentle sea breeze and already the beach was looking very busy. The promenade had steps leading down on to the beach at various intervals. We walked close by the hand rails in the hope of spotting the girls, avoiding the deck chairs and the ice cream on the floor. The sea again was very calm, with boaters launching their craft amongst the bathers. The sea even looked blue today.

'Alf, it should be a good day for the beach, especially if we can spend some time with the girls. Plus tonight we have the "Big Star Show". I'm looking forward to that. I think the Tornados will be great and I want to hear the Karl Denver Trio singing "Wimoweh". Who are your favourites?'

'It has to be Billy Fury, but I like Marty Wilde as well. Marty's new record "Jezebel" is a good one. There's also a comedy act on, a bloke named Chick Murray from Scotland. Are we going to posh up and wear our new clothes again?'

'I don't see why not, Alf. If we wear the same outfit, we can pretend we're part of the show. Could be that Larry Parnes himself will be there and might recognise us. Who knows, we might get to meet one of the stars.'

We continued to amble along the prom still looking over the rails every so often. But look as we might, we couldn't track the girls down. Eventually we came up to the Britannia Pier entrance and decided to go in and do the walk to the end; the girls could have been in any one of the penny arcades.

We passed people sitting in deck chairs, relaxing in the sunshine, taking in the sea air whilst looking out to sea, others eating ice creams and some holidaymakers simply catching up on lost sleep. Older men had their handkerchiefs knotted at the corners and placed on their heads as sun protection, whilst the women had their frocks pulled up above the knees getting their legs tanned.

Walking on, we saw a group of people looking down over the railings on to the beach. We walked over to see what was happening. The tide was right out at this stretch and the sand looked dark and dirty. A number of kids, covered head to toe in this oily black, mud-like sand, were digging down into it with their hands. The man next to me, as well as some others, was dropping coins down, which sank into the mud.

Turning to me, the man said, 'These kids are called the "mud larks". Well that's the name everyone calls them,' he continued. 'If you drop a coin down, it will disappear into the mud and they dig down, waist high in mud if needs be, to retrieve it.'

'Rather them than me,' I replied.

Moving on we came to the penny arcade amusements, lights flashing everywhere from the many machines. A noisy place, especially when the machines pay out, dropping the coins into the tray.

'Alf, let's have a play. I've got a pile of pennies, we can have a go on the one-arm bandits and the pinball machines.'

After playing the machines for a while, and inevitably losing our money, we found the noise level was getting too much. People were screaming when the machines paid out and anyway, the girls were not in here, so we decided to move on.

As we moved further along the pier, you could see the sea between the cracks in the wooden boards rushing in underneath. The tide had turned, so the 'mud larks' had better watch out. Further on the fishermen were castings out their lines. I think it was some sort of competition as to who could cast the lead weight out the furthest. The smell of fish bait greeted you and there were squashed crab claws everywhere. Having reached the end of the pier, where the theatre is, we decided to turn round and head back down to the promenade and continue our search further along the prom.

As we got to the end of the pier, Harry caught sight of Sandra, one of the girls we were searching for, buying an ice cream from a stall on the prom. We both ran, hoping to catch up with her before she descended the steps back down on to the beach.

'Hi Sandra,' said Harry, tripping up in his haste to get to her. 'We have been looking for you lot most of the morning.'

Sandra, wearing a swimsuit and a shirt-type top to cover up somewhat, said 'Why don't you both come down on the beach and join us? I can see you've got your towels with you. The water is quite cold though, if you are thinking of a swim.'

At that the thought of a cold swim was not on my agenda. I hate being cold, anyway, it has a tendency to shrivel up your manhood.

'Well we've already been in and had a quick dip, thanks, I

said, 'but we will come and have a chat.' I asked Sandra if Joan was going to be there.

'We're all there,' replied Sandra.

So we trudged our way over the sand, tiptoeing round all the deck chairs and sand castles until we arrived where the girls had set up camp. Joan was stretched out on a towel, looking absolutely fabulous in a yellow and white polka dot, high-waisted bikini, with sun glasses on, reading a copy of the 'Teen' magazine. Ruby was busy covering her legs with sun cream, whilst Mavis was chatting to a family who were sitting behind.

It was a typical scene with everyone enjoying their time on the beach. Close by, I noticed a mother spreading butter on bread for their sandwiches, her kids dribbling ice cream over everybody and the father pumping up the primus stove to make tea.

Joan eventually stopped reading and peered over the top of her magazine.

'Hello, Alfie,' she said, 'it's good to see you. Sit down and relax, we can have a chat. The suns getting hotter. It's coming up to midday, take your top off. You can tell me what you've been up to.'

We all found space to sit down, Harry and I did remove our shoes and socks, so as not to look too out of place, and settled down to enjoy the afternoon sunshine. I got my wish wanting to see Joan in a bathing costume and I did eventually take off my shirt, taking in a deep breath at the same time, puffing my chest out.

I settled down lying beside her. The air smelt lovely as I inhaled a mixture of her scent, sun cream and the sea air. Harry sat down beside Sandra and asked her what they thought of the 'Big Star Show'.

'Absolutely great,' replied Sandra, sitting up quickly. 'All the singers were good, especially Marty, he has a fabulous voice, in fact, I wet myself when he came on. You'll enjoy it, Harry, when you go.'

'Hopefully, but I'll try not to wet myself.'

Ruby piped in with, 'I screamed that much when Billy came on, that my throat's now quite sore.'

'Sounds as though we are going to enjoy it then,' said Harry. 'That's if we can hear the music above the girls screaming.'

We spent the afternoon chatting about our favourite singers and what we liked to do in life in general, the act of going for a drink we all agreed on. My eyes, however, were generally focused on Joan's body, strong looking and well-proportioned. I got the feeling that she wouldn't take any prisoners if you messed with her. As I lay beside her I watched her breasts gently moving up and down in the sunshine, slowly stretching her bikini top as she breathed in and out. I edged real close and whispered in her ear, 'You're so beautiful it hurts to look at you and not touch.'

Joan turned her head, looked at me over the top of her glasses and without saying anything, simply returned back to her magazine, my comment falling on stony ground.

Was that a comment too far? How I would have loved to climb aboard, feel her breasts push up against me with every intake of breath, gently kissing her lips and waiting for the arousal time bomb to kick in. It wasn't going to happen here on the beach with hundreds of people about but it had to happen with someone, at some time on this holiday. I needed a conquest and to hit the ground running when I got back home, hopefully into the arms of Moira. Joan lowered her magazine and turned her head towards me again, saying, 'Do you have a steady girlfriend, Alfie?'

'Well, not really at the moment. I try not to get too involved,' I said, thinking chance would be a fine thing.

In a whisper and with a twinkle in her eye, Joan lowered her sunglasses down a little and continued with, 'What you're saying is, you love them and leave them.'

'That's right.' Little did she know that I woefully lacked any serious form of love making. Could she be the one to put things right?

The girls took turns going in and out the sea to cool off, and Harry and I took enjoyment watching them drying off in the late afternoon sunshine. With time moving on and needing to get ready for the show tonight, we arranged to see the girl's the following night around 8pm for a drink down at Paddy's Bar. We left the girls to it and made our way back to the digs, stopping off on the way for some fish and chips. There's something good about eating fish and chips out of the vinegar-soaked paper. We ate them with gusto as we continued walking along the promenade.

Chapter 16

Washed and shaved, we continued to get ready for the evening, putting on yet again our matching outfits, and we were about to leave the room when there was a gentle knock on the door. I opened the door to find Mrs Cassington leaning against the wall, looking rather special in a tight-fitting floral blouse and black skirt, and looking straight past me she said, 'Harry, I have that same problem with my table lamp; you know the one I thought you'd fixed before. Do you think you could take another look at it in the morning?'

Harry thought, if being engaged as an electrician is the only way to get shagged round here, then so be it, and she has a way of making you perform at your best, so if needs must, then needs must ...

'Sure, Mrs Cassington, I will take a look at it first thing in the morning. At the moment we are off to see the "Big Star Show" at the Windmill Theatre and we are late already, so we have to get a bit of a move on.'

'Oh right, well lads, don't let me delay you any longer. See you in the morning, Harry.'

'Yes, first thing.'

As we left I said to Harry, 'You must be mad, mate. We are supposed to be on holiday, you're not an odd job man, fixing her electrics free of charge. You want to ask her for a reduction on the room rate.'

'She's ok,' replied Harry. 'She hasn't got a husband, so she needs someone to sort her out. It won't take me long, if it's anything like the last time. A pull and a shove, a tickle here and a tickle there and her lights will be glowing again in no time.'

On the way to the theatre we were passing Lilly's café, and as I looked in I could see Mr Parnes sitting at his usual table in the window, sipping his coffee, reading a newspaper.

'Harry, that's the manager in there, Mr Parnes. Shall we go in and say hello?'

'Yes I've clocked him. Sure we can go in. If he remembers we're here to see the show tonight, we may just get invited to go back stage.'

Before we had even closed the door, Mr Parnes looked up immediately and recognising us, beckoned us over to join him at his table.

'Hi lads, how are you two doing? Join me, sit yourselves down.'

'That's nice of you, but we can't stop, we are going to see the show tonight. We just wanted to say hello and thank you again for the tickets,' said Harry.

'That's ok, boys. I tell you what.' Mr Parnes reached out of his top pocket a white card and wrote something down.

'After you have seen the show go to the ticket office with this card and the security guy there will show you the way to the dressing rooms at the back of the stage. You'll find me there and we can all have a drink, and I'll introduce you to Billy, if that's ok with you, lads.'

Our eyes lit up at the prospect of meeting up with the stars. We thanked him and left.

When we got outside, we both looked at the card he had given us. It read, 'Larry Parnes, Impresario and Personal Manager to Billy Fury – Tommy Steel – Marty Wilde.'

Harry said, 'look at his address: the Penthouse, Derwent House, Cromwell Road, London.'

'The Penthouse,' I said. 'The Penthouse. He lives in a bloody penthouse, that's special. You've got to have loads of money to own an apartment on the top floor.' Turning the card over it simply read, 'back stage pass x 2.'We were so chuffed with our invitation as we made our way across the road to the theatre.

Entering the theatre, the atmosphere was electric with people waiting in the foyer. We had never seen so many girls dressed up to the nines in their best clothes. Lots in miniskirts and high boots, bouffant hair styles, full make-up. The lads had made an effort too. The place was buzzing as we jostled our way past the stairs leading up to the circle, then through the doors into the auditorium, and down to find our seats in the stalls. The sound of everyone expressing their excitement was amazing, all sat waiting for the deep red velvet curtains to open and the show to start.

Harry and I moved along the row looking for seats J11 and 12. When we sat down, the girl sitting next to me suddenly poked my arm and, with a mouthful of gum, leaned over, saying, 'Are you two boys with the show?'

'What made you say that?' I replied.

'You look as though you are, you're both wearing the same clothes.'

Her mate sitting next to her, sucking on an ice cream, piped up with, 'You look like dancers.'

Dancers, I thought, cheeky cow. But thankfully before I had

a chance to answer the lights in the auditorium went down, except for the lighting on the velvet red curtains, which slowly opened with the band kicking off the music. First up were 'The Windmill Girls', arm in arm, strutting their stuff, high kicking as they danced across the stage. A singer named Daryl Quist was introduced and appeared from the back of the stage, a Canadian I think, just starting out. He looked as though he's just left school, he looked so young. Anyway, he sang a couple of songs and went off. A chap named Alan Field came on next, introducing the 'Vernons Girls' a glamorous singing trio who sang a number called 'Lover Please', followed by another song from Daryl. Although there was some screaming from the girls with his act, it was nothing compared to the sound when Marty Wilde came on, especially when he started singing 'Jezebel' followed by 'Teenager in Love'. That had the girls wetting themselves, and I bet there were a few teenagers in the audience whose hearts had been broken after a quarrel and looked to the stars for guidance.

The first half finished off with Marty, the Vernons and Windmill Girls all performing together, to the great delight from the audience. As soon as the interval came, Harry turned to me, saying, 'Come on, let's go to the Starlight bar at the rear, give my ears a rest. Unfortunately, I'll have to get the drinks, you don't look old enough.'

'Ha ha, piss off. But that's ok if you're buying.'

When we returned to our seats, the gummy girl next to me said, 'You are with show aren't you? My mate thinks you are.'

Knowing we were going back stage I couldn't help but lie, saying. 'Yes we are with the show, but not actually performing on the show, we are personal assistants to one of the stars.'

She turned her back and started whispering to her mate. My nose just got longer and longer.

The second half kicked off with 'Peter Jay and the Jaywalkers', an instrumental group, followed by the comedian Alan Field. Only us lads, seemed to laugh at him. Next up was the 'Karl Denver Trio' singing some of their hits including 'Wimoweh'.

A number of other acts came on before finally, the reason why most of us had come, on came the fabulous, the one and only Billy Fury together with the 'Tornados'. Well you couldn't hear the first song above the screams as Billy got into his stride. Dressed in a silver grey suit, white shirt and dark blue tie he gave us songs such as 'Halfway to Paradise', 'I'll Never Find Another You', 'Jealousy' and the hit single from his film 'Once Upon a Dream'. Screams ensued throughout Billy's performance and at the end the entire company came on for the 'Mardi Gras Finale' Everyone in the audience applauded or screamed. With the show over, as is the norm, everyone made a dash for the exits.

'Alf, that was a great show, wasn't it?' said Harry as we left our seats.

'Fabulous show, I thought, and you could tell everyone else had enjoyed it. Look at them, they're all leaving with smiley faces. I heard the two girls that were sitting next to you say on the way out that they were going round to the stage door to catch a glimpse of the stars when they come out to ask for their autographs.'

'Perhaps they will ask for ours, when we come out.'

'Yes, in your dreams, Alf.'

We made our way to the ticket office in the foyer and showed the woman sat behind the screen the card we had been given by Mr Parnes. The woman looked at it and then at us. 'Oh right,' she said as she handed me the card back and pressed a call button.

A moment later a security guard quickly appeared on the scene, and having been put in the picture said, 'You best come with me then, lads.' He then took us through a door, down a long fusty smelling corridor, up a flight of steps to a door marked 'Private Theatre Staff Only'. He opened the door and said, 'Now lads, just go in and you will find Mr Parnes in Billy's dressing room, fifth door on the left as you go down the corridor.'

It was quite noisy as we made our way down the corridor, with people talking, music playing in the background, everyone no doubt unwinding after their performance.

We slowly walked on. Some doors were open and we couldn't help but slow up and stare in. There were people in a state of undress, taking off their costumes and hanging them up ready for the next show.

'Alfie, did you see who was in that dressing room? The guy with his feet up on the dressing table, bottle of beer in one hand and a fag in the other.'

'Yes, I saw him,' I replied, 'That's Mike Sarne, he's one of the singers appearing on the show at the Britannia Theatre on the end of the pier. He's had a number one hit. He probably comes over to have a chat and relax with the other stars from here.'

We reached the fifth door on the left, which had Billy Fury's name on it, right in the middle of a silver star. Very appropriate, I thought. Harry, having straightened his tie, went to knock on the door, but the door suddenly opened and one of the Vernons Girls came out. Holding the door ajar for us, she said 'Just go in, boys,' and walked off.

We walked in and immediately saw Mr Parnes sat on a sofa in the corner of the dressing room, cigarette in one hand and a drink in the other. Closing the door, I noticed lots of clothes hanging up along one wall, including the shiny silver grey suit Billy had been wearing on stage and a row of shoes underneath. Billy was sat on a stool at his dressing table, now in casual clothes, and was looking in the mirror, cleaning off his make-up. The mirror had lights all the way round the edge, lighting up his tray of make-up and the general clutter on the table in front of him.

'Hello, boys,' said Mr Parnes. 'Come in, take a seat and let me introduce you to Billy.'

At this, Billy swung round on his stool, smiled and nodded to us.

'Billy,' Mr Parnes continued, 'this is Alfie and his pal Harry, I met them the other day and promised them a tour backstage.'

At this Harry stepped over and shook Billy's hand, saying how much he had enjoyed the show; Billy made no comment, just smiled as he continued to remove his make-up with balls of cotton wool. I rubbed my hands on the sides of my trousers, as if meeting royalty and I too walked over and shook Billy's hand. It was the softest of all handshakes. His eyes seemed vacant somewhat, a look not helped by the eye shadow he was still removing with his other hand. Again he said nothing, just simply turned back round to pick up more cotton wool.

'It's really good to see you again, Mr Parnes,' said Harry. I just nodded in agreement.

'As I've said before, boys, call me Larry. You make me seem very old. Whilst I think of it, and before I show you round to meet other artists in the show, providing they are still here and not down the pub, how would you two boys like to go to an all-stars cricket match with us tomorrow?'

Stunned for a moment, I looked at Harry. He in turn looked at me, both wondering if we just heard that right. A cricket match with Billy Fury – I don't believe this.

'Did I hear you right,' I said, 'you want us to come to a cricket match?'

'Yes,' said Larry. 'If you two have nothing better to do, we have a charity cricket match on tomorrow. Lots of stars are taking part, or coming to give their support. It's the Britannia Theatre verses the Windmill Theatre. Weather permitting, it could be a good fun day and quite relaxing, especially if the sun is shining, but I have ordered it.'

Before I had a chance to answer, Harry jumped in with 'Sounds great, yes we would love that. If you would write down the cricket grounds address for us, we will be there.'

Larry took a pen out from his inside coat pocket and wrote down an address. When he gave me the piece of paper he said, 'This is where we are staying during the summer. It's a house that's just a short drive down the sea front, towards Caister-on-Sea. Some of us are stopping there for the summer season; it's a big house, big garden, plenty of room and very quiet.'

'It must be a big place if you're playing a cricket match there,' I said.

'Sorry Alfie, let me explain. The cricket match is being played at the local cricket ground, but I would like you and Harry to come to the house first and we will go on from there. I will drive us there in my Jaguar, but I would like you to accompany Billy in the back of the car. We need to make a big impression when Billy arrives at the ground. There will be lots of people there and it's important for Billy to look the star that he is, so we need to turn heads when we arrive, you understand.'

Harry and I just sat there; mouths again wide open, not believing our luck.

Larry continued, 'Please wear the same clothes, if that's ok with you boys?'

'Yes, that's ok with us, Larry,' I said, suddenly feeling part of the scene and thus dropping the Mr Parnes bit.

'What time would you want us to arrive at your house?' said Harry.

'Ten o'clock sharp if you will, bails on at ten-thirty.'

At that Larry got up and said to Billy that he would see him later, adding, 'Now watch how you go in that car of yours.' Billy never turned round, just looked in the mirror, smiled and said, 'I'm only going to drive along the prom a couple of times and then I'll see you back at the house.'

We were given a brief look round backstage and got introduced to some of the other stars of the show, and then we arrived at the rear of the theatre by the stage door exit. Larry thanked us and said he would see us tomorrow morning at ten.

Well, we both felt so important as we left through the stage door, not only because of the invitation but also our joy at being greeted by a crowd of young people, who were waiting to mob the stars as they left, getting their autographs. We smiled at them as we pushed our way past and noticed gummy girl and her mate were there. She shouted out 'I know them.' Telling everyone close, 'we've sat by them two, they are with the show.'

Our egos were getting bigger by the minute. What with the theatre tickets, back stage passes, involvement with the stars of the show and now a day out tomorrow to watch a star-studded cricket match, it really couldn't get any better.

As it was quite late now, we decided not to go for a drink but to make our way back to the Sea Breeze for an early night. Walking along, I said. 'This is proving to be a great holiday, mate, full of twists and turns.'

'Too rights, what with this cricket match tomorrow and then meeting up with the girls in the evening. It can't be bad, providing the girls turn up that is.'

'I've been thinking about the girls, if only there weren't four of them.'

'Yes, but unfortunately girls do tend to stick together.'

'Yes I know what you mean, it's just that, I was hoping for the chance to get Joan to myself.'

'I don't think that's going to happen.'

'Have we established that you would know what to do, if you did?'

'Ha bloody ha.'

Chapter 17

The next morning, as I lay in bed, I could hear Harry making a noise as he moved around in the bedroom, piffling.

'Harry,' I said, as I rolled over to look at him, 'What are you messing about at, why are you up so early?'

'It's not that early, besides I have promised Mrs Cassington I'd take another look at her light, don't you remember? Anyway, I'm taking a bath first, and then I'll see what's wrong with her light.'

'Best get a move on then. I will need to go the loo soon.'

'Yes I will.'

'I do remember Mrs Cassington saying she would treat us to a cup of tea one morning, in bed. You could remind her that tomorrow will do.'

'I wouldn't bank on that.'

'No, you're probably right, all talk and no action is Mrs Cassington.'

Harry just smiled and looked for his toilet bag. I rolled over to go back to sleep for a while longer.

Harry, with a towel round his neck, descended the stairs to the bathroom, switched on the light and used the loo before running himself a nice hot bubbly bath, using someone else's toiletries he found on the bathroom shelf. Bubble bath that he thought might just have belonged to our vision from heaven,

Virginal Rose. Slipping down into the water, shrouding himself in a hot steaming mist, he still had Rose in his thoughts. As he lay there, his thinking changed to Mrs Cassington. Had he read her right? Was sex on the agenda again that morning, albeit, wham bam thank you mam, or could there be a genuine problem this time with her light, their last sexual encounter just being a one off? However, on cue to his thinking, Mrs Cassington opened her door to the bathroom and whispered, 'Is that you, Harry, taking a bath?'

Sinking further down in the water, he answered equally quietly, 'Yes it is, I will be right with you, once I've finished in the bathroom.' There was no reply.

Seconds later, Mrs Cassington appeared before him, stood by the side of the bath with full make-up on, hair done up on top and totally naked, but for her right hand covering her vagina, as if holding on to some modesty was necessary, at least for the time being. Her other hand was outstretched, inviting Harry to take it. Harry quickly sat up and helped her step into the bath. Without saying a word, she then pulled Harry up, both now paddling in the lovely hot soapy water. Taking the soap, she rubbed it all over her breasts and carried this on down to the top of her legs. Dropping the soap in the water, she then placed Harry's hands over her proud nipples. Harry responded, cupping both her breasts, feeling the fullness of them. Smiling at him, she put her finger on Harry's lips as she raised her right leg up, wrapping it round his body. Harry was not to say anything, as she slowly slid his one hand off her breast and then further down her soapy body. In the sexual heat, Harry's arousal time shortened by the second and instinctively he was left in no doubt as to what she wanted him to do next.

Was there no end to her sexual appetite? Her body trembled slightly when he tenderly touched her clitoris and began to circle it with the tip of his finger; Harry was no stranger to the pleasure zone. He felt her hand instantly close around his very erect penis and they continued to caress each other, looking only into each other's eyes, without a word spoken. They stifled their excitement as best they could, eventually burying their faces in each other's necks. Then it was a case of stand and deliver, and deliver it was, having both relieved themselves from the tension they were under.

Mrs Cassington had taken control completely during this sexual interlude and not one word spoken the whole time. Harry helped her get out of the bath and now, with his tank empty; he sank back down in the water, his eyes still focused above the bath on Mrs Cassington's body as she reached her bedroom door, looking just as beautiful from the back. This mature, fully experienced woman who took what she wanted, when she wanted it, turned and blew Harry a kiss, smiled, then returned back into her bedroom.

Whilst he had enjoyed being seduced by an older woman, he thought how unreal it all was. He had not experienced anything like it before, despite his many conquests, and it convinced him that women get more sexier, more desirable, more sexually demanding the older they get, seeking new ways to get sexual fulfilment and, if required, take charge to get it.

Harry would remember Mrs Cassington forever, in fact, every time he ran a bath that is.

Now exhausted, but in another way refreshed, Harry quickly finished off in the bathroom and returned back up to the bedroom.

'It's about bloody time,' I said. 'You take ages in the bath, it's a wonder you haven't shrunk.'

'Actually, in a way I have, but that's another story,' replied Harry. 'Anyway it's your turn now. We need to be on our way to Caister by nine-thirty, we've got a cricket match to attend.'

Having both got ready for the day, dressed in our new clobber, we went down to breakfast. Walking in to the dining room we said good morning to the other guests, including Rose and her parents. Having perused the breakfast menu, we both spent a few moments ogling Rose's petite arse as she bent over, reaching for the sugar off the next table. We ordered our usual breakfast and we only had a short time to wait before our waitress brought it to our table, and I again noticed that Harry had got two eggs again. Before the waitress left, I said, pointing to Harry's plate, 'Why is it he has two eggs and I've only got one?'

'You will have to ask Mrs Cassington, she has done the cooking this morning,' answered the waitress. 'I feel it's just a mistake; if you want two eggs I will bring you another one.'

'Don't bother, we haven't got time now, we have to get a march on this morning. I just wondered that's all.'

Harry, who didn't say a word, tucked into his breakfast and we quickly finished off to get out for the day, not wanting to be late arriving at Larry's house.

'We won't use the van this morning,' said Harry, 'although this house we are going to may be a distance. I think its best that we catch the bus, Larry may not take too kindly to having an old bull nosed van parked on his drive.'

'Yes, you're absolutely right,' I replied. 'It's bound to be a posh house; we won't be doing ourselves any favours, especially parking the van next to his Jag.'

We made our way down to the promenade and caught the bus towards Caister. The conductor said he would tell us when we were at the start of all the posh houses, and that's where we should get off. It wasn't long before he gave us a shout and we got off the bus and walked along until we came to the address that Larry had written down for us. It certainly was a large house; old brick with big bay windows and a long drive. In front of the house we could see four big expensive looking cars and a sporty kit type car with no roof, silver in colour with black seats.

'I bet that's Billy's car,' said Harry, as we walked past it.

On reaching the front door, I used the knocker and we waited. Music could be heard playing and then the door was opened by a lady with a pinafore on, who asked us in. Upon asking for our names she said to please wait in the hall, and that she would let Mr Parnes know we were here.

'She must be the housekeeper,' Harry said quietly, as the woman disappeared through a door, closing it behind her. We could hear music being played all round the house, someone playing one song upstairs and another different one from the lounge, everyone with different tastes I guess. The music from the lounge suddenly stopped and a minute or so later, the housekeeper came back into the hall saying, 'Please, do go in. Mr Parnes is in the front lounge. He will see you now.'

Walking into this huge lounge, sofas and soft furnishings everywhere, we saw Larry busy putting his coat on and calling for Billy to get a move on.

'Good morning, boys,' Larry said, eyeing us both up and down. 'Thank you for coming, you both look great. Now what I would like you to do is to sit in the back of the Jag with Billy in the middle, it's all about making a good impression for when we arrive at the ground.'

Larry put his arm around my shoulder as we walked back into the hall, saying, 'It's going to be a great day, that's providing Billy gets a bloody move on.'

Larry told his housekeeper that there would be guests coming for drinks that evening and could she put out some picks and things.

'Billy,' he shouted again, as we passed the stairs. 'Please hurry up, we have to go; we will be outside on the drive.'

Larry unlocked the doors on his gleaming Jaguar, dark grey in colour with reddish leather upholstery and a walnut dashboard. He opened the back door and asked me to jump in and slide across. I climbed in and sank into the leather upholstery, soaking up the smell of the leather as I scanned the dashboard in front of me. Billy arrived on the drive, smartly dressed, walking quite slowly with no sense of urgency at all.

'Come on, Billy,' said Larry, 'we really do need to go.'

He got in the back of the car and sat in the middle, not saying a word, followed by Harry slipping in the other side. Larry fired up the Jag with the touch of a button, all the gauges coming into life, and we set off to the cricket ground for this charity cricket match.

All the way there, Billy didn't speak at all, not even to say hello, just sat slightly forward, eyes glued to the front windscreen. We in turn kept quiet and felt just privileged to be taking a ride with this famous guy and being part of the pop scene. I looked over Larry's shoulder in amazement at the various toggle switches on the dashboard; it had no less than six dials as well, all giving loads of information about the car.

This was the poshest car I had ever been in, it was also very quiet inside and I felt very important as it purred along.

After a short ten minute drive we arrived at the Yarmouth cricket ground. There were security people on the gate but they allowed Larry, who they recognised, to drive straight through and down to a car-parking area. You could see lots of spectators sitting on the grass around the boundary, taking in the morning sunshine, waiting for the cricket game to begin. The small grandstand overlooking the green was already filling up, I guess with theatre people of one sort or another. Some of the stars were already wearing their cricket whites and everyone was for sure enjoying the lovely morning sunshine that Larry had ordered.

Larry parked his Jaguar deliberately in the front of the parking area, opposite the grandstand, making sure everyone would see us as we got out of the car. Harry opened the rear door, got out, keeping the door wide open, allowing Billy to also slide out making his big entrance, closely followed by me.

'Boys,' said Larry, as we all walked towards the grandstand. 'Could you walk up to the changing rooms with Billy, then cut across to the grandstand and grab your seats, you'll enjoy a good view of the match from up there and I'll see you later. I need to have a chat with someone. Billy will sit where he wants to once he's got changed into his cricket gear.'

Harry and I took our seats, looking down at some of the singers and dancers on the front row, some we recognised from last night's show, both of us feeling as pleased as punch as we sat in the sunshine waiting for the game to start. Billy came over from the direction of the dressing rooms, having changed into what looked like brand new whites; he made a move to sit in between one of the Vernons Girls on the one side and Marty Wilde on the other. Most of the stars from the two theatres were there and it wasn't long before both teams walked out. With a flip of a coin from the umpire, the game got under way, with Britannia Theatre opening the batting.

The Windmill side soon realised they were a man short on the field; someone hadn't turned up. After debating who had cried off, the match organiser asked around if someone wanted a game. A moment later, who should step up to the crease? No other than another great entertainer, Joe Brown, singer and fabulous guitarist, performing at times at the Britannia Theatre, and was in fact their twelfth man if someone from their side didn't turn up. However, the Britannia side said they were eleven up and didn't mind him playing for the opposition, as it was all in fun and, more importantly, all for a good cause. Joe borrowed some whites, quickly got changed, and joined the other fielders.

A scrappy game of cricket took place, you might say, with very few runs taken over the next hour, but with lots of fun and laughter, not only out on the wicket, but also from the spectators. The umpire, who was also in fits of laughter most of the time, was doing his best to stick to the rules of the game. I'm not sure if the umpire, with his flat cap on, wasn't Chick Murray the comedian. It would explain the laughter coming from the crease in between overs. The game progressed, with some of the stars taking it very seriously and others doing the best they could. However, not one of them I would say would be picked for any national team, not in a month of Sundays. Nonetheless the Britannia side had entertained us all morning, but their last man in was caught and bowled and were now all out, having scored a respectable sixty-seven runs. The game then broke up for afternoon tea.

At tea we got treated to sandwiches and cakes. Harry and I tucked in, whilst being questioned from time to time by people wanting to know what we did and how did we come to know Larry. Harry was full of bullshit and glossed over the questioning, not giving way to letting anyone know that we were really just hangers on for the day, as you might say.

Returning to our seats, the game quickly got underway, with the Britannia fielders trying to decide where to stand. Daryl Quist, a singer on the show with Marty Wilde, strutted out to open the batting for the Windmill team with us all cheering them on. Marty played really well and with some runs on the board he was eventually bowled out. Everyone clapped and cheered the big man as he walked back to the pavilion. Now it was Billy's turn to bat with Daryl the other end. Billy, in his immaculate whites, adjusted his pads, turned his shirt collar up and with his bat raised in the air strode out to the crease with everyone cheering him on. Acting like a professional cricketer, Billy marked out his middle stump as a point of reference for receiving his first delivery, I think he must have played this game before. It wasn't a fast first delivery and he played it to his offside for a quick short run, much to the delight of the crowd. Daryl was next to take his gloves off, having been caught out with the next ball, after hitting the ball up to the gods. Billy progressed, putting a few more runs on the board, but it wasn't long before he got run out by one of the stage crew in a bit of a mix up. He returned to the pavilion to a huge round of applause, having scored eleven runs, including a boundary. Over the next hour, Britannia soon reduced the batting order down and it was looking a close call as to who would win.

I looked at the score board and the Windmill lads now had a commendable fifty-six runs, needing a further twelve more runs to win, but with only two left to bat it was going to be a tight game and could go either way. Two overs later, Britannia got another wicket and with only a further seven runs on the board for the Windmill boys, the game was on a knife edge. It was now down to Joe Brown, the last man in and a guitarist from the Tornados, the other end, to get the rest of the runs to win the game.

Joe, already padded up, strutted out to the wicket, turning round at one point, acknowledging the shouts of encouragement from the crowd, he ran his hand over his spikey hair before giving us all a wave. At the crease Joe marked out middle stump and scanned the field, plotting out a course for the ball to go. Despite the banter at the crease and the shouting from the Britannia side, trying to put Joe off his game, two more runs were added off the next two balls, leaving Joe at the crease for the next over. There were now shouts and cheering coming from all sides as the bowler was about to deliver the next ball.

Now, taking advantage of a slow ball, Joe's raised his bat with anticipation and with great gusto connected with the ball, right on what they call the sweet spot, and lifted the ball right up into the air, sending it searching for the boundary.

All eyes were on the ball as it seemed to hang in the air, and despite a tremendous effort to get there by a fielder it just dropped over the boundary for a six, to loud cheers from all supporters, who by now were on their feet. Joe had won the game for the Windmill Theatre and everyone cheered as both sides came off. Joe even got pats on the back from the

Britannia team. Everyone in the grandstand stood up and clapped both teams in and a big cheer went up for Joe, which he acknowledged by raising his bat, the champion of the day was all smiles as he entered the dressing room.

All the players then got changed and after a few celebratory drinks, with much discussion, we again escorted Billy back to the Jaguar and Larry drove us back to their big house on the sea front in Caister.

On arrival at the house Larry pulled up and looked over his shoulder at us in the back, asking if we would like to go in for a drink and a chat. Well you couldn't have wiped the smiles off our faces. After quickly accepting, we all went in together. We followed Larry into the lounge and Billy disappeared upstairs. Harry and I made ourselves comfortable in the huge leather armchairs in the lounge, and Larry went into the kitchen. I looked around the room – lots of everyday pictures adorned the walls, but nothing personal in sight, I guess because the house was rented.

I leaned towards Harry and whispered, 'It's been a great day out, mate, hasn't it? We didn't expect to be doing this before we came away on holiday, did we?'

'No, we didn't. It's been great watching the cricket match, but remember we've already had a few drinks, so take it easy. We have arranged to see the girls tonight, remember.'

'How could I forget that?'

Larry arrived back into the lounge with a tray of glasses and removed a full bottle of whisky from the biggest drinks cabinet I have ever seen, full of bottles of one drink or another. Adding ice from an ice bucket, he poured whisky into each glass and said, 'What do you have with your whisky then, lads, as it is, on ice or with soda? or perhaps you would you like something else?'

'We both like dry ginger, if you have some,' said Harry.

'Sure, no problem, I've got everything in here. Before we come here for the summer, I always get the housekeeper to get all the stocks in for the season and we never run out, despite here being an open house.'

Larry raised his glass, saying, 'Cheers lads, you have done a good job today, and I hope you have enjoyed yourselves?'

Harry and I raised our glasses and I said, 'Yes we have, and the Windmill lads winning the game as well just made the day.'

'Yes, Billy and Marty played well, but Joe was the saviour of the day.'

Larry then put on a record and topped up our glasses with more whisky, placing a bottle of Canada dry ginger on a table, to help ourselves. He then sat down in one of the beautiful leather armchairs. Amazingly, the record he put on wasn't a pop record, but something rather more classical. We sat enjoying our drinks, and a little later Billy returned to the lounge having changed his clothes yet again. He put on a little blue jacket over his white shirt and said to Larry that he was going out for a drive around.

'That's fine, Billy,' said Larry, 'but be careful in that car of yours and no stopping to talk to your fans. You need to be on time for the show tonight.'

Billy said 'ok,' combed his hair, turned his collar up on his jacket and left the room.

Larry, turned to us saying, 'I don't like it when he goes out on his own. I tell him not to stop for fear of people mobbing him, but he does like driving his car around with the top down so his fans can see him.'

'I thought the open top car outside was his. It's a nice sporty looking job,' I said

'Yes, I gave him that as a bonus to use throughout the summer season here in Yarmouth, seeing as he's top of the bill. You know, lads, I have got some of my friends coming round later for drinks, perhaps you would like to stay and join us. We always have a good time. In fact if you want to, you can both stay for dinner afterwards and even sleep here for the night. Harry can stay in the only spare room we have and Alfie, you can sleep with me.'

I just sat there staring into my drink, somewhat stunned; my brain was trying to work out Larry's last remark. With my brain still in overdrive, I took a sip of my drink and looked at Harry, he looked at me and we had a moment of silence as we both sat completely still, sipping our drinks. Did we read that invitation right? Was Larry simply being friendly? Others would give their high teeth to be mixing it with celebrities. Or were we getting into something we ought not to? Whatever it was, we were not expecting that kind of personal invitation. Without really answering, Harry said, 'Right, Alf, as much as that sounds like a good invitation, we really must be going, don't forget we have an appointment later with the girls.'

'Yes. Of course, today has been so exciting. I'd forgotten what we were doing this evening, it's probably the whisky. It's gone to my head.'

I was unsure if I had understood correctly regarding Larry's intentions for the night. Anyway, Harry's remark would certainly have put us out of the running.

'Another time then perhaps,' said Larry, as he rose up from his chair.

Harry and I put down our empty glasses, and followed

Larry into the hallway.

Larry thanked us for our support today and as he shook our hands and repeated the invitation to come for dinner anytime, as we would be most welcome.

'Larry, we would love to come back another time, but sadly our holiday is nearly over,' said Harry.

'You're from the Midlands aren't you?'

'Yes we are,' replied Harry.

'Well, remember, boys, Billy will be appearing at the Hippodrome in Birmingham later in the year and we stay at the Albany Hotel, so you have my card. Please give me a ring and we can get together for a drink in my suite.'

'Sounds great, appreciate that, thanks,' I said on leaving.

As we walked down the drive, I was still thinking about what Larry had said. He'd certainly been very friendly and seemed happy to be in our company. We carried on walking away from the big house, down towards Great Yarmouth town itself, looking for the bus stop.

'Harry, did I get that invitation to stay the night wrong? Was Larry just being nice and hospitable or what?'

We both stopped and Harry looked at me, shook his head and carried on walking.

'What's that supposed to mean?' I said, as I caught up. 'Why are you shaking your head?'

Harry stopped and turned to me, saying, 'What Larry was saying, mate, was that he fancied your arse more than mine, and probably after a bite to eat and a few more drinks he was probably going to take you to his bed and show you a thing or two.'

Harry spelling it out like that made me come all over in a cold sweat.

'A shirt lifter you mean,' as I again caught up with him.

'Who knows, he could be, but I may be wrong, anyway, I don't think we should run the risk of any embarrassment.'

'Well that was a bit of a close shave then, I didn't think Larry was that kind of a bloke.'

'Look Alf, he may not be, he's certainly been a gentleman and given us a good time today. There are all sorts of people in the pop world, but with some you just have to decide which path to take.'

Chapter 18

We eventually caught the bus back to Great Yarmouth, continuing to chat and reflect on the fabulous day's events.

'You know what, Harry, if all I get out of this holiday is an offer from the same sex, I think I will go mad. I could go on through life being celibate and become a Trappist monk, wanking in silence. Having said that, it's not been good for you either, has it mate? In fact, both of us could end up going home without having had any sexual contact on this holiday.'

'That's right, mate, this holiday from a sex point of view is sadly lacking,' replied Harry, lying through his teeth, as he recalled his encounters with the lovely, can't-get-enough Mrs Cassington.

As the bus made its way down into Yarmouth, back to more familiar surroundings, we decided to go to our usual place for something to eat. Taking food on board would be the best thing to do, seeing as how we had supped a few drinks today, with more to come tonight.

Lilly's was buzzing, but we managed to get a table. It was our usual waitress and she took our order for egg beans and chips and then asked how we were both doing.

Harry briefly gave the waitress a rundown of the day's events. She couldn't believe we had spent the day with Billy Fury and wanted to know more.

'You are lucky boys,' said the waitress. 'How did that come about then?'

'Well, it all began with us being invited by that Mr Parnes, the man who sits in the window, to an all-stars charity cricket match, which was played today. He drove us and Billy Fury to the ground, where we joined other stars for the game.'

'You were in the same car as them?' said the waitress. 'Wow that would explain why we haven't seen him in here today. We like Mr Parnes, flamboyant and gay, but a very nice man.'

Now she tells us, I thought.

'Done well for himself as well,' the waitress continued. 'He told us he used to be in the rag-trade, but that wasn't satisfying enough and involvement with rock and roll was inevitable. Although some artists that come in here refer to him as "Parnes, Shillings and Pence" because of the way he does business.'

We enjoyed our evening meal at Lilly's and having put some food in our bellies, followed by mugs of tea, our heads had started to clear somewhat from the whisky Larry had plied us with, so we returned to the Sea Breeze guest house to get ready for tonight's meeting with the girls.

Entering our bedroom, Harry said he was going to get changed and put on something more casual. I agreed, so we both took turns to have a quick wash and brush up. Trousers and a short-sleeved shirt are all that one needed. A splash of the Aqua Velvet aftershave I'd taken with me and a touch of Brylcreem to flatten the sides of my hair down and I was good to go. In anticipation, I remembered to take my packet of Durex just in case, although the way things had worked out so far on this holiday, I didn't think they would get used somehow.

A warm barmy evening greeted us as we stepped outside

the Sea Breeze. Harry checked the van was still in one piece, remarking that he hoped it would start up ok for our journey home. We made our way down to the promenade and joined the throng of people already enjoying an evening stroll along the prom. As we passed the Britannia Pier, the evening walk, together with the smell of the sea air filling our nostrils, had cleared any remaining fuzziness in our heads and we headed straight on down to Paddy's Bar.

Approaching the bar we could see Mary and Bert were in their usual spot, wearing the proverbial summer hats and sun glasses, enjoying the last of the day's sun.

'Hi, you two,' said Harry. 'Have you both had a nice day?'

'Hello, lads, yes we have. We've done absolutely nothing, which at our age is having a ball of a time, said Mary, breaking into a chuckle.

'What about you two, what have you been up to?'

'Can we join you and I'll tell you all about it?' said Harry.

'Sure. Sit down, we have saved a couple of chairs,' said Bert.

'Harry, you sit down' I said. 'I'm just going to see if the girls are inside.'

'Right ok, get the drinks in then, mine's a brown and mild.'

'Bert, can I get you and Mary a drink?'

'No son, we are ok, just sort your selves out.'

'Fine, I'll be back in a minute.'

Harry proceeded to give Mary and Joe a brief rundown at what we had been up to during the day, whilst I went inside to find the girls, if they'd decided to come that is. They weren't in the bar or lounge, so I got a couple of pints of beer and returned to join Harry and the others outside.

As I put the drinks down on the table, I could have guessed

that Bert would tell us his latest joke. Mind you it's good to kick the night off with some banter and a joke or two, especially whilst we waited for the girls to arrive. I was going to be very disappointed if they don't turn up.

Bert, however, did not disappoint and kicked off with his latest joke …

'A woman and her husband interrupted their holiday to go to the dentist.

"I want a tooth extracted and I don't want any pain relief, gas or otherwise. We're on holiday and I'm in a hurry," said the woman.

The dentist was quite impressed, saying, "You're certainly very brave. Which tooth is it."

The woman looked at her husband and said "Show him your tooth, dear."'

Everybody fell about laughing at that one, a good clean joke as well. Upon which the girls, bless them, suddenly appeared out front, looking all tanned and healthy. They really did look stunning, all dressed up to the nines in their short smart summer frocks, especially Joan I thought. She had a lemon-coloured outfit on, buttoned down the front, with a wide black shiny belt which she pulled in tight to show off her trim waist and boobs at the same time, the whole outfit finished off with a pair of white sandals.

'You all look fabulous,' said Harry, as he pushed the chairs around to accommodate the four of them, making sure he was sat next to Sandra. We introduced Mary and Bert to the girls and once the girls had decided what to drink, Sandra went inside to get them. We settled down on Sandra's return and, with us all relaxing, Harry and I started to tell them what had transpired at the Big Star Show the night before and the subsequent events of today at the cricket ground.

'Hold on, you two,' said Joan, 'you mean you were socialising with the people on the show, mixing it with the stars?'

'You bet!' I said. 'We had an invitation from Mr Parnes, or should I say Larry, to go backstage after the show and meet some of the stars, especially Bill Fury. In fact we ended up in Billy's dressing room.'

'How fabulous,' said Joan.

Harry followed up with, 'We also got invited to an all-stars cricket match today as well, and the best thing was we got a lift to the cricket ground, sitting next to Billy Fury, in his manager's car. A big four-door grey Jaguar with leather upholstery, dials and switches everywhere. You couldn't even hear the engine running when it started up.'

'What's he like?' said Ruby, one of the girls.

'Who?' I said.

'Heaven forbid, Billy Fury,' continued Ruby.

'Good looking, but you know that all ready. He's quite tall, but not as tall as Marty. He must be well over six foot. Billy's very quiet, doesn't say much at all, in fact I don't think he said more than few words to us. He spoke all the time to his manager.'

'So what happened today at the cricket match?' said Bert's wife.

Harry and I both started to speak at the same time in our excitement, Harry carried on telling them about the match, who had scored what and which team had won.

Turning to Joan afterwards and changing the subject, I asked her if she was enjoying her holiday.

'We are, thanks; it's been great fun being with the girls,

but some of the blokes we've met on holiday are right dorks, present company excluded of course. So tonight I'm hoping to get a bit sloshed and have a good time. What about you two? You've done ok, mixing it with the stars, but have you met any girls since you've been here?'

I couldn't tell her that we've had no luck whatsoever, despite the fact that when we first arrived we were staying at Selbourne House, the house of ill repute, with plenty of women about, who would have performed for us no doubt. However, it was not something Harry and I could handle, or would want to. Even now staying at the Sea Breeze, which was a really nice place, the only girl you would love to have sex with reckoned she was not old enough, stupid girl. Then there's our landlady, Mrs Cassington, widowed and very attractive, dressed to impress, middle aged but still very sexy, but who probably preferred more mature blokes.

Answering Joan, I said, 'Yes, we've met a few girls, but Harry and I like to play the field and move on. We don't like to get too involved.'

Chance would be a fine thing, I'm thinking, as we downed more drinks.

The time by now had gone way past Mary and Bert's bedtime and they decided to bid us a fond farewell, shook our hands, thanked us for our company and hoped to see us next time we were in Great Yarmouth.

'Good night, you two,' said Harry, 'and next year don't forget to bring your joke book with you, you've been great fun.'

'Yes right,' said Bert, 'good night then everyone, sleep tight, God bless.'

They left, strolling down the prom arm in arm, Mary still

clutching her handbag and totally devoted to each other, both having enjoyed another night in their beloved Great Yarmouth.

More drinks were ordered, all of us getting merrily pissed as we enjoyed another night on holiday, laughing and joking, all in good spirits, to use the pun.

Was it my imagination or was Joan sitting closer to me every time she took a drink, finally leaning over and whispering in my ear, 'Alfie, you tell fibs. I don't think you have been seriously out with many girls, have you?'

I just stared at my drink for a moment and then Joan, with her mouth now right next to my ear, said, 'In fact, listening to you, I think you are still a virgin.'

'A virgin? What, me, still a virgin?' I whispered back. My face must have been as red as a beetroot. I didn't really know how to respond to her and took another sip of my drink.

'I'll have you know I have a girlfriend back home, waiting for me.'

'How long have you been going out with her then?' said Joan.

'Well actually, I've only just met her and we haven't been out on a date yet. She's a friend of friend and we all go around together.'

'What's her name then?'

'Moira.'

Still whispering in my ear, Joan continued, 'Well if you've only just met Moira, and always in the company of others, then I still think you are definitely a virgin.'

My face must have been bright red now, and with Harry now well pissed, holding forth with the other three girls, Joan got up, kicked off her sandals and told the others that we were just taking a walk on the beach for a paddle. Grabbing my hand, she pulled me up from the chair, saying, 'I need to stretch my legs.'

So after taking my shoes and socks off, we left the others to it and both set off across the road on to the promenade, continuing on down the steps, straight onto the beach.

As we headed towards the sea, the sand became firm underfoot. The tide, having gone out ages ago, was well on the way back in.

After a few more yards, Joan took my hand, saying, 'Well we've got our feet wet now, let's head back closer to the prom and walk up to the pier.'

Her hand in mine felt really nice as we strolled along the beach, like a proper couple. The air was still warm with just a little breeze coming in off the sea as it continued to roll in, glistening in the moonlight. We slowly walked along adjacent to the promenade, which was now all lit up with its trailing coloured lights, strung out between the lampposts, disappearing into the distance.

Joan stopped for a moment, turned to look at me, and standing close, took my other hand saying, 'Sorry if I put you on the spot back there. I didn't mean to embarrass you. I'm a little older than you and I'm able to read people quite well. I just expressed my thoughts. It was wrong of me.'

'It's not a problem,' I replied.

Although she had summed me up right, I continued by saying 'I'm happy just being with you tonight. You are lovely and a great fun girl to be with.'

No way was I going to admit to being a virgin, but she was absolutely right. I was embarrassed, and not having sampled any form of sexual delights on this holiday, my situation was now getting to me.

'Right then,' said Joan, 'I'm in need of some summer loving. Let's enjoy the rest of this evening and carry on up to the Britannia Pier. When we get there, though, you being a virgin is not going to be an issue for you anymore.'

I was stunned for a moment, thinking, summer loving, did I hear her right? Is she going to take me in hand, perhaps walking towards Utopia? My brain was now in overdrive, trying to compute. What if I didn't measure up, underperformed or made a fool of myself perhaps? What Joan had just said went through my brain over and over again as we moved further along the beach. Not wishing to act like a child on the way to the sweet shop, I said nothing. I took in deep breaths of sea air and continued our conversation with, 'Not many people left on the beach now, Joan.'

'No there isn't, but that's just as well, don't you think?' At that she let go of my hand, and proceeded to run the last few yards to the pier.

'Come on, Alfie,' she shouted.

The only people about were a couple walking their dog and a few late night swimmers, and having arrived at the pier, Joan took my hand, saying, 'We need to slip under the iron work, the sand there will be completely dry.'

'The tide doesn't come up this far then?' I asked.

'Not quite, looking at the seaweed line on the beach it doesn't.'

Having now got right under the pier, Joan sat down on the sand and with an outstretched hand pulled me down towards her.

I sat down beside her; the lights from the promenade were

just enough for me to see Joan unbuckling her shiny black belt and remove it.

This is it, I thought, I'm not dreaming, it's happening. I'm about to have my first lesson in love making. Having removed her belt, Joan lay back and, resting her head on the sand, she looked at me, saying, 'Alfie, I've had a couple of relationships, so let me help you.' She turned towards me and started to undo my trouser belt.

My body was already starting to react to the situation as she undid my belt and unbuttoned my fly, then finally pulling me round to face her. With her legs now either side of me, she lay back on the sand, leaving me to stand up and slip my trousers down.

With my heart now racing away like an express train, I couldn't help thinking that the last time I had this experience was with Moira in the cloak room at the church dance.

Joan started undoing the buttons from the top of her dress. As she did so, the first thing she revealed in the low light was her lily white bra, adorned with a pretty pink bow in the middle. What was running through my mind now was where I had put my Durex. Which trouser pocket were they in? This was made worse by me now having my trousers down round my ankles and my pants halfway down. I fumbled around in the pockets of my trousers whilst Joan continued undoing her buttons on her dress.

Joan, being the switched on girl that she was, said, 'Alfie I know what you are looking for, but you don't have to worry, I'm on the pill.'

At this I stopped searching, kicked off my trousers and pants and watched Joan just undoing the last button on her dress, which she slowly opened wide. She had no knickers on, setting the fireworks off and her tanned body highlighting the special white sacred part of her body, where the bottom of her polka dot bikini bathing costume had been. She then opened her legs, pushing the sands to one side as she did so. I knelt down between Joan's legs, staring down at her for a moment. Everything looked so beautiful and neat; my eyes slowly moved upwards at the rest of her body, all of which was glowing in the low light.

Joan raised her knees slightly as I lowered myself down, the smell of her scent was fresh, fragrant, not too strong. I slowly lifted up her loose-fitting brassiere, until her proud nipples slid out from underneath. With my fingers now dug into the sand either side of her body, I felt her firm breasts push up against mine and with my cock now in overdrive, I was hoping I didn't ejaculate prematurely all over her. Restraint was certainly needed; after all, I'd waited for this moment for far too long and wanted it to last as long as possible.

Then I felt Joan take hold of my penis and raising her hips slightly, she gently inserted it into her wet vagina. Joan sucked in a breath and squirmed as she opened up; I felt her warm muscles gripping me as I slid slowly and fully in. I couldn't have imagined how beautiful this new experience was going to be. Joan placed her hand at the back of my neck, pulling my head towards her.

I stroked her silky cheek with my lips as I buried my face in the side of her neck. Through my lips I could feel her pulse rate increase as I began kissing the side of her neck. This moment was for real; I was making love for the first time. Making love with Joan, a girl I had only just met and yet was giving me my first shag.

The sound of the sea, filtered through my ears as the waves came in, doing its gambol before crashing on to the shore – how romantic I thought. Music could be heard coming from the pier above us; it was a song by Johnny Burnette singing 'Dreamin''. How apt was that?

Except I wasn't dreaming, and my search was over now. With Joan's fingers now gripping my bottom tightly, I immediately started a rhythm of slowly moving back and forth, and with every push seemingly being at the same time as the incoming waves crashed on to the beach.

I couldn't hold back any longer, I was now rushing in faster than the sea was coming in. Hopefully I was satisfying Joan, considering my amateur status and not having been there before. Joan started quietly moaning and then breathing heavily, whilst at the same time, digging her nails deeper into my bum. It seemed like only seconds had gone by before, with one final thrust on my part, we both surrendered with huge groans and sighs of relief. At that moment I lifted my head and smiled down at Joan, slowly withdrew and rolled back over on to the sand, us both feeling united as I held her hand whilst lying there. As I looked up, rays of light came down through the gaps in the pier decking. Footsteps could be heard from people leaving the show at the end of the pier, no doubt having been well entertained.

We both lay there looking upwards, and after a few moments Joan turned on to her side and, looking at me, she said, 'How was that then, Alfie boy?'

Squeezing her hand, I replied, 'Perfect, just perfect. This evening has been the best evening I have ever had in my whole life.'

Joan gently pulled down her bra, returning her beautiful

breasts to their nests, and began to button up her dress, adding, 'Well you can go and sow your oats elsewhere now, welcome to the club.'

'It's all been amazing, I will always love you to bits for what you've done, the problem is, you will be going home tomorrow and I'll be just a summer memory.'

'Do you never go back to the same place twice then?'

I was like an excited puppy at the thought of coming back here next year. I smiled at her saying, 'There's always a first time for everything.'

'That's right, there's always something different to see and try.'

Joan's words will be embedded in my brain forever.

Having both got dressed, and with the tide now only a few feet away, we thought it best to quickly make our way back down to Paddy's Bar to join the others.

When Joan and I arrived back, people were already spilling out of the bar and lounge to go home. I could see two of Joan's friends, Ruby and Mavis, still in the terraced area, curled up together on a bench, obviously feeling a little worse for drink. Harry and Sandra were nowhere to be seen, so we sat down, still holding hands. A moment later I looked across the road and saw Harry and Sandra coming towards us, swaying back and forth, laughing as they crossed the road from the beach, barefooted and holding their shoes.

'Hello, you pair,' said Joan. 'You both look a little tight, what have you been up to?'

'Just been for a paddle in the sea, it's amazing how warm it is for this time of night,' replied Sandra.

'Paddling in the sea, you little liar. You mean you've been for a wee wee!'

'How did you guess?' laughed Sandra.

'Easy, your frock is still tucked into the back of your knickers.'

'Oh shit,' replied Sandra, giggling as she pulled her frock down at the back.

We all fell about laughing.

I looked at Harry, and as he turned round to pull up a chair there was sand all down his back. Somehow I don't think Sandra had been on the beach just for a wee. Knowing Harry, they must have been at it as well.

Ruby and Mavis had started to stir on the bench and Joan gave them a gentle shake, saying that it was time they all went back to their digs to crash out.

'We will walk you lot home, then,' said Harry, in somewhat of a slurred voice.

'You don't have to do that,' said Sandra.

'Alf and I insist. We would love to walk you home, no arguments.'

So after all agreeing it had been a great night all round, we walked the girls back to where they were staying. It wasn't that far away, just a little way up the prom, which was just as well, fortunately, because I don't know who was holding who up as we all walked along arm in arm.

Everyone embraced, all agreeing to come back to Great Yarmouth at this time next year, with Ruby adding, 'Bring two of your mates with you next time though, as well.'

'That's right,' added Mavis, 'We'll always turn up at Paddy's.'

That wouldn't be a problem, I thought. Eddie from the dairy would be up for it, he'd soon give Ruby some of his Gold Top.

I took Joan a little to one side and quietly thanked her for giving me a good time, especially for awarding me my 'Non-Virginal Badge'. She just winked and held me tight, kissing me lightly on the lips for the very first time. Strangely enough we hadn't kissed on the lips all evening, especially when we made love. Perhaps this was a girl that just got down to the business in hand, no foreplay, no attachments, no relationships, just a nice shag, or summer loving as she calls it, at the same time being selective as to who she has sex with.

My hand slipped out of Joan's, and having said our goodnights and wishing them a safe journey home tomorrow, Harry and I left and made our way back to the Sea Breeze guest house.

'Well, are you going to tell me then?' said Harry.

'Tell you what,' I said, as I picked up the pace to get back.

'Did you or didn't you with Joan?' Harry said, frustrated.

'I did, I did, mate. I am now complete, and I can't wait to get back to see Moira and give her one.'

'You lucky bastard.'

'I am, but you struck lucky with Sandra as well, didn't you?'

'No I didn't. Just happened to be the wrong week for her, but we did have a good snogging session and a fumble on the beach. Her tits are amazing.'

'Well, mate, I'm sorry shagging has not been on the agenda for you this holiday. I thought you might have got off with Mrs Cassington. You know she fancies you. She's not young, but still very attractive and extremely sexy with it.'

'She is,' replied Harry, 'but I think it's all show.'

Harry, not wishing to add anything more to that conversation, followed up by saying, 'With the girls going home tomorrow, what about us going home as well, perhaps first thing in the morning rather than hanging around for another day?'

'Yes I'm happy with that, plus the weather tomorrow is going to be quite cloudy at times. But remember we said we would take a holiday present back for the girls.'

'What kind of present?'

'I'm not sure, but it would be nice to take them something back.'

'Well, by the sound of it you're going to give Moira something anyway.'

'Yes I am, but seriously, I want to take her back a nice present.'

Arriving back at the Sea Breeze rather late, Harry struggled to find the door key, but eventually found it and opened the front door. We both crept in, trying to be as quiet as we could, not wishing to disturb the other guests. As we started to climb the stairs, a door up the hallway opened and, talk of the devil, out came Mrs Cassington.

'Hello, you two,' she said, standing there in her black nightdress, her tanned cleavage in full view. 'Has your night on the town been a good one?'

'Yes it has,' I replied. 'A very good night. Brilliant in fact.'

'Sorry we are so late coming in,' said Harry. 'By the way we've decided to make our way home tomorrow after an early breakfast, if that's ok?'

'That's fine, boys; it's been nice having you stay here at the Sea Breeze and you are most welcome to come again. Perhaps, Harry, you could pay me for your room in the morning?'

'Sure,' said Harry, smiling and knowing what her terms of payment might possibly mean.

We said goodnight and continued on up to our bedroom.

Chapter 19

The following morning, as I woke up raising my head from beneath the bed clothes, I could see that Harry had already got up; he certainly likes to get down in that bathroom first thing.

Harry, of course, had probably bathed and was doing his duty by paying Mrs Cassington for our accommodation. I decided to get dressed first and have breakfast, then use the bathroom later.

A little while later Harry came back up the spiral staircase from the bathroom, saying that he had got up early, bathed and sorted out the bill with Mrs Cassington. 'I've paid her in full,' he said, 'so as soon as breakfast is over we can get underway.'

'That's ok with me, but as you've been a long time in the bathroom, I will have breakfast now and use the bathroom afterwards, whilst you pack your suitcase. I've already packed mine.'

We went down to breakfast for our last time. Most of the residents in there had finished their breakfast and were sipping their last cup of tea, whilst listening to the music playing on the radio and probably, like us, some of them having the same idea of making an early start to the day or their trek home.

Rose, 'The vision from heaven', looked at us and smiled as we sat down at our table.

After a while Rose turned round, and asked, 'Are you boys going home like us today?'

'Yes we are,' I said, as I rearranged my knife and fork ready for breakfast.

'Did you enjoy your last night in Yarmouth?' she continued.

'Yes we did,' replied Harry. 'In fact, last night we had a great time, there was a crowd of us. You'd have liked it.'

I thought I knew what was in Harry's mind.

'Are you going to come back to Great Yarmouth the same time next year, perhaps stay here at the Sea Breeze?' Rose asked.

Harry piped in immediately with, 'We might just do that, and especially as you will be sixteen next year.'

At that, Rose's parents turned round and gave us both a look of disgust, and, adding further to our embarrassment, the song on the radio, as if by magic, changed to Neil Sedaka singing 'Happy Birthday Sweet Sixteen'.

Rose looked at us, smiled and turned away to finish her breakfast. Her parents mumbled something at each other, still glancing at times in our direction, giving us the evil eye.

I felt like saying, 'Don't come bathing at ours next time your pipes burst.' Well, they could, as long as they brought Rose.

The waitress came over to us, placing down a teapot and a rack of toast on the table and said, 'The usual full breakfast, lads?'

We nodded in approval and then carried on talking about our journey home.

'Let's hope the van starts up, Alf. We haven't used it for a week; if it doesn't then it will mean the battery has run down, so you will have to crank the engine over with the starting handle, whilst I operate the throttle. I hope it does start though, my head is still beating like a big bass drum this morning.'

'Well you and Sandra did sup some booze last night, mate, but what a great night it was. Pity about Sandra's timing though.'

'Yes it was. Still it was good night for you though, wasn't it, you lucky bugger.'

'You're right. It was unexpected as well. I can honestly say it was the best time I've ever had and I can now go home feeling I've come of age.'

'You certainly have. Now, when we've finished breakfast, I will pack my things whilst you take a wash and get ready.'

'I shall miss these breakfasts, Harry,' I said, 'but I'm still none the wiser, as to why you always end up with two eggs and I only get one.'

Harry smiled and said he was a bigger lad; they probably thought he needed more protein.

We left the dining room and returned to our room for the last time. Harry got on with his packing and I went down the spiral staircase to take my bath, also for the last time.

Having bathed, I quickly started to get dressed when suddenly the door opened that led to Mrs Cassington's private apartments. Mrs Cassington stood in the doorway, still dressed in the black nightdress she had on the night before.

'Hello, Alfie,' she said, 'sorry to intrude. Are you getting ready for the journey home?'

'Yes,' I said, quickly doing up the belt on my trousers. 'Do you want to use the bathroom, because I've nearly finished.'

'No I don't actually. It's my bedside lamp, Alfie, it doesn't seem to be working again and I wondered if you could take a look at it for me?'

'Sorry Mrs Cassington, I'm no good at electrics. You need

to talk to Harry about electrics; he's pretty useful at that sort of thing.'

'Oh right, not to worry then. It will keep for another day.'

At that Mrs Cassington smiled, gave me a wink and closed the door, and I quickly returned back up the spiral staircase to the bedroom.

'You've been quick,' said Harry. 'I haven't finished packing yet.'

'Actually, Mrs Cassington opened her door and asked me to do a job for her. She has a problem with that lamp again and wanted me to fix it for her, the cheek of it. I wasn't having any of that; I'm here on holiday not here to work.'

Harry started laughing and said, 'Quite right, mate, quite right.'

'What's funny about that?'

'Oh it's just that I thought I had fixed that lamp. It obviously needed tweaking a bit more.'

We both left the bedroom and, having loaded up the van with our suitcases, Harry reached out a can of oil and topped up the engine for the journey home. Then, having closed the back doors, Harry jumped into the driver's seat to see if the engine started up. The engine gave a slow growl, turned over a few times and then died. It was a case of reaching for the good old starting handle. I fitted the handle through the hole in the front bumper to connect with the crank and turned it real slow like until I could feel the compression. Harry turned the ignition on and, remembering to have my thumb in the right position so as to not break it on kick back, I gave the handle a good pull up. Sure enough, the engine came into life, at first with a bit of a murmur, then coughed and spluttered before Harry quickly pumped the accelerator a couple of times to keep it going. Moments later, the engine started to tick over nicely and I quickly removed the starting handle and jumped in the van, whilst Harry kept the engine running.

'That's it then,' I said. 'It's time to go home.'

As Harry selected first gear, I dropped the side window down and looked out to find Mrs Cassington standing in the porch of the Sea Breeze. She gave us a wave and said, 'It's been great having you both stay here. Please come back again soon.'

'Do you know what, Harry? We couldn't have asked for a better landlady and a better place to stay at. I still think she fancies you. I reckon, if you'd played your cards right you might have scored with her. Mrs Cassington might be getting on a bit, but you would agree, she's still very attractive and very fit looking for her age.'

'You could be right, Alf, and for all I know she might be red hot in bed. They say the older ones are the best shags. Anyway, it's a bit too late to find out now.'

He then let the clutch out with a jerk and we set off, the engine groaning for a while as we got up to speed for the long journey home.

'Well that's our holiday over,' said Harry, 'but we've had a good time, Alf, haven't we? The holiday has certainly made a man out of you and we've certainly got a lot to talk about when we get back home, meeting Larry Parnes and all the stars.'

'Yes, it's been great; I'm trying, though, not to think about Joan and I certainly won't be talking about our time spent here with the girls. My only thought when we do get back is to quickly get it on with Moira. Thinking about what we have done during the week, starting with our encounter on the way here with the Gypsy, Silvanus. Meeting Joan and the girls on the prom, the first day we arrived. Then the problem we had with the first accommodation Mom had booked us in to, the notorious Selbourne House.'

'Yes Alf, what a dump that place was, a guest house with a posh name, prostitutes, drunken Yanks and the offer of a pint of mild with your breakfast. Are you going to tell your mom about the place?'

'I will have to; she will ask anyway and I think it's best to. When I tell her about how nice the Sea Breeze guest house has been, especially the cleanliness and how good the food has been, she'll be happy.'

We headed on down for our last drive along the prom. It was awash with people strolling along in the morning sunshine, people out just for the walk, others rushing to get their place on the beach for the day. I must admit, as much as I want to go home and see my friends, it's always sad to leave.

'Oh shit,' I said loudly to Harry. 'I've just remembered, we haven't got the girls a present.'

'Bloody hell, Alf, I'd forgotten about that. The problem is, I haven't really seen anything that might be a good present to take back either. What do girls like, unless you think a stick of rock or a "Kiss Me Quick" hat is ok?'

'Hardly, but I think we should make the effort, take some sort of present back. It will stand us in good stead with the girls.'

At that, Harry pulled over and stopped the van, leaving the engine running, both of us just sitting in silence for a moment. The engine nicely ticked over whilst we both threw ideas at each other, both of us being really at a loss as to what to buy the girls.

'I tell you what,' said Harry, suddenly turning the van round and heading back in the direction we had come from, 'we'll go back to that chemist shop.'

'The chemist shop, what on earth are we going to get from there?'

'When we were in there the last time, whilst you were pratting around buying condoms, I noticed that they sell all sorts of smelly things, we can buy something like that for the girls. Anything in a bottle and fragrant, girls will like.'

'I hadn't thought of that, good idea. But nothing too expensive, I've only got so much money left.'

Harry pulled the van up right outside the chemist shop and, leaving the engine running, we both went in to have a have look and to hopefully get a suitable gift to take back.

Who should be at the counter serving? No other than the girl I bought the condoms off. Harry looked round the perfumery shelves, picking up various items, smelling them and placing them back. As for me, I just gazed at things in general.

Meanwhile, the girl assistant behind the counter was giving me the eye and that certain smile; it was obvious that she was recalling my embarrassing moments when I was in last time.

'You won't want any protection today will you?' she said to me with a cheeky grin.

How could she know we were heading home?

'It's going to go cloudy for the rest of today,' she continued.

That cleared that remark up.

'You're possibly right, anyway we are going home today. What I'm looking for is a present for my mother, something with a nice smell to it.'

She smiled at me and beckoned me down to the other end of the counter. Picking up a floral decorated box, she removed the lid, revealing a selection of small individually wrapped soaps. 'These smell really nice and are very personable, plus they are better quality than Woolworths and nice for young and old alike.'

I think she knew who they were for; she was just being very nice. I liked them to look at and, picking the box up, they did have a nice collective aroma. Putting the lid back on, I turned the box over to see the price, which was ok as well.

'Yes, its perfect thank you. I will take it.'

'Would you like me to wrap it for you?'

'Would you? That will be good, thanks.'

Meanwhile, Harry had sorted out his gift for Lynda as well. Both gifts were wrapped up and, having both paid, we were keen to get back on the road. On leaving the chemist shop, the girl assistant said to me, still wearing her cheeky grin, 'I'm sure your girl will like the soaps.'

Chapter 20

We got back on the road and, with the van chugging along like a good one, we slowly made progress as we listened to the radio, stopping only once to let the engine cool down and deciding to stop for a longer break when we were somewhere near Huntingdon. The old van had done us proud, albeit that it bounced around a bit and was very sluggish on power when it came to the hills. It wouldn't pull the skin off a rice pudding at times, but we get there. Travelling through the green countryside had been lovely and made a change from the built-up area of bricks and mortar where we both live and work. We carried on chatting about the holiday, trying to remember some of the jokes that Bert came out with, but like all good jokes, it's hard to remember them.

'I can remember the one about the Vicar,' said Harry.

'Which one is that?'

'Vicar welcomes the people into the church, for the morning service. A loose woman comes up to him with a very revealing top on. Vicar says, "You can't come in here dressed like that." The woman says she has a divine right to come in. Vicar says, "You have a divine left, but you still can't come in."'

The morning progressed with the van plodding along nicely, only having to stop once more to top up the radiator. The roads were very quiet, very few hold ups, but when eventually we reached the outskirts of Huntingdon we started to slow up. Cars and a truck or two were going slow up front, obviously held up with something.

'Look at all these cars in front of us. Can you see what's holding us up?' asked Harry.

'I can't, could possibly be a tractor, but more likely a broken down car or something, or it might be road works.'

'Could be a good time to stop and have a break then,' Harry replied.

'Hardly, the queue of traffic is long enough as it is.'

We slowly moved up position, still unable to see what was backing up the traffic, as the road was so narrow. Eventually, when we got to a bend in the road, we could see what the problem was, some kind of horse-drawn cart holding us up.

'Don't tell me it's a Gypsy caravan that's holding us up,' said Harry

'I'm not sure; I think it might just be. Perhaps Huntingdon is the home for travelling families. Whatever it is, we have a long queue behind us now.'

As we got a little closer, we could see it was indeed a Gypsy caravan, or should I say Vardo, remembering the encounter we had with our Gypsy friend on the way to Great Yarmouth.

'Hey, it couldn't be Silvanus could it, out and about on his travels again?'

As we got closer, moving up the queue one at a time, we somehow knew it just had to be Silvanus; you could not mistake the style and colours of the wagon. We moved further up, until there was only one car ahead of us. When that car in front overtook we would be right up behind, then we would see if it was our Gypsy friend.

As the car in front made a dash to overtake, Harry shouted out, 'It is him, it's Silvanus. Look what's swinging from the back of it, it's the hurricane lamp, the thieving bastard. I knew it was him.'

'It is,' I said, 'I'd recognise that lamp anywhere.'

'Well we need to overtake and see for sure if it's him, then we can be certain the lamp is the same one.'

'I tell you, it's the same one, it's got to be and I want it back. My old man will give me a right telling off if we go home without it.'

'How the hell are we going to get it back then?' said Harry, as he looked for an opportunity to overtake.

'Well, even if we can get him to pull over, which in itself would be difficult, I don't think either of us would have the nerve to ask him for it back.'

'So what are we going to do then?'

'I know,' said Harry. 'We will overtake, firstly to check if its him, and if it is, when we get round that bend up ahead we will pull off the road and wait for him to come by.'

'What then?'

'I don't know yet, I'm thinking.'

A horn sounded from the truck behind us, obviously someone getting impatient and wanting us to overtake and get a move on.

'I've got it,' said Harry. 'We'll do as I've said, overtake, and when we're round the bend, we'll pull off the road. Then, when Silvanus comes past, you creep up behind him, climb up on to the back of the Vardo and retrieve the lamp.'

'You want me to run into the road in front of the other traffic and do that?'

'It's your father's lamp, mate, after all he's only going at a snail's pace. Just do it, I will wait and be ready with the engine running to follow up.'

'Let's hope he doesn't recognise the van.'

We eventually pulled out and slowly passed the Vardo. It was Silvanus alright. He was sitting very still with the reins in his hands, his head bowed, probably asleep, accepting that his horse, Patch, knowing the area so well, would just keep on going to their next stop.

Now was as good a time as any to get our property back, so we motored on ahead, having both agreed on the plan of attack. Other vehicles followed us. We carried on round the bend and pulled off up a track, turned round and lay in wait for Silvanus to come by.

'Now, when he comes past, walk behind it for a while and then climb on the back, facing the vehicle that may be following, you will look part of the scene. Then, when the following car starts to overtake, grab the lamp and jump off. I will be coming up behind at some point to pick you up.'

At that we heard the sound of the horse's hooves thumping the tarmac as it came plodding round the bend. Silvanus was still sat there with his head bowed. So I did what Harry suggested, walked on behind the Vardo. Then, a minute later, I jumped up on the back and the hurricane lamp was in my hand.

I sat there just enjoying the ride, for a moment, on the back board. Eventually, Harry came up right behind and I slipped off, jumping back into the van as it crept along.

'It's back with us again, mate, safe and sound. Mission completed.'

'Well executed,' said Harry. 'Now we have to pass him again, lower your window down, and when we overtake I will sound the horn, whilst you wave the lamp out of the window.'

This we did, Harry hit the horn briefly and I swung the lamp outside the window as we slowly came alongside the Vardo. Silvanus looked up immediately at the sound of the horn and, sensing that something was alongside, looked to his right, and being the cute one, he realised at once who we were and seeing Alfie waving the lamp, immediately knew what had just taken place. After we passed him, I looked in the door mirror glass to see behind, I could see Silvanus shaking his clenched fist at first, then, with a broad smile on his face, simply waved at us. With no harm done and with the lamp back where it belongs, any thought of a bollocking from my old man when we got home was no longer on my mind.

Having got through Huntingdon and feeling chuffed with ourselves, having rightly got our own back on Silvanus, we decided to have a quick break before continuing to push on home, whilst listening to the sound of the Drifters singing 'When my little girl is smiling' albeit on low volume as the spare battery was by now fading fast and in need of charging.

'That song reminds me,' said Harry. 'Are you looking forward to seeing Moira?'

'I sure am. I will be smiling when I see her, in fact after we unload the van lets pop over to Lynda's house and see if she's in? She may ring Moira to let her know we are back and maybe, possibly, meet up tonight or tomorrow.'

'How do you know she will want to see you?'

'If my encounter with her in the Church rooms is anything to go by – she will.'

We arrived back to Harry's place around tea time and

backed the van into the yard at the back of the store. Harry's dad came out and greeted us with a smile, asking if we'd had a good time, but at the same time giving his van a quick look over, no doubt checking that we hadn't put a few dents on it during the holiday.

'Yes we've had a great time,' I said. 'Eventful you might say, but a good holiday, and we met some really nice people as well.'

'That's good,' said Mr Richards. 'I hope though, that you pair didn't sow too many seeds whilst you were there. You don't want anything coming back to bite your arses now, do we?'

I thought straight away of what Joan had said to me, being on the pill.

'Dad, give us a break,' said Harry, 'we know what we are doing.'

Turning to me, Harry said, 'I tell you what, mate. You go over and see if Lynda is in, whilst I start to unload the van.'

As I left the yard and turned round the corner, who should I see over the road but Moira, walking with a fella, tall and with some presence, both going in the direction of Lynda's house. I stopped in my tracks and felt the bottom of my stomach drop out. I'd only been away a week and she has someone else in tow. I did a U-turn and returned back to the yard, Harry could see by the expression on my face that something was wrong.

'What the fuck's up, you got indigestion or something?'

'I've just seen Moira heading towards Lynda's house with another chap.'

'What sort of chap?'

'What sort of chap? A fucking good-looking chap, that sort of chap.'

'Well, when the cats away the girly mice will play,' said Harry.

'Oh! Thanks, mate. I wasn't expecting that. It really took the wind out of my sails. I'm feeling right gutted now and I've only been back five minutes.'

'What did you expect? You're away on a shagging initiation holiday and you think Moira should stay indoors, waiting for you to get back?'

'No sympathy from you then, a fine mate you are. I might as well give you a hand now to unload the van.'

We emptied the van of our stuff and got it ready for any trips it might have to make. I collated all my things together and popped them in the back of the store to take home.

'I hope you've left some petrol in my van,' said Mr Richards. 'It's got some deliveries to make after the market tomorrow.'

'We have, Dad. It's got a quarter of a tank left and as you can see the van's unmarked. It drove well, only had to top up the oil and water on the journeys.'

Harry closed the back doors of the van. I thanked Mr Richards for letting us use it and went to close the gates. To my surprise, who should be standing at the entrance? Lynda and Moira, waving to us with big grins on their faces? I wasn't sure how to react towards Moira after seeing her with this handsome fella, but we both slowly walked over to greet them, with some reservation on my part.

'Hi, you two,' said Lynda, 'have you had a good time on holiday then?'

'Yes, we have, weather was good, accommodation good, eventually that is. And we met some very nice people as well,' said Harry.

'Meet up with any girls then?' said Moira, looking in my direction.

Thinking of the fact that Moira had got another guy in tow, I replied directly with, 'Yes, we did meet some girls. In fact we spent some time with them. Nice girls actually.'

Seeing both girls suddenly lose their grins, and now with their heads lowered somewhat, Harry piped in with, 'What Alfie means is four girls actually, but all very much above board, no hanky panky, just good fun. More importantly, we've met a number of really interesting characters whilst on holiday, from landladies at both end of the spectrum, to an impresario, to famous pop stars, and not to mention a really scary Gypsy guy.'

Spectrum, where did he get that word from? Still, I couldn't stop thinking of this guy with Moira and had to ask. 'Anyway, who's your latest flame then?' I said to Moira.

Looking a bit puzzled, Moira said, 'what do you mean, your latest flame.'

'The fella I saw you with over the road, a little while ago.'

'You mean the tall good looking fella, smartly dressed?' Moira said with a devilish grin.

'Didn't really notice actually what he looked like. I only caught a slight glimpse of him, anyway you're free to do what you want.'

'Well you don't have to fret, Alf, that good-looking fella is my brother.'

With that knowledge, my stomach quickly returned to normal and I felt a right idiot for jumping to conclusions.

'Yes, he's my older brother on his way to meet his girlfriend.'

'Sorry, Moira, for thinking otherwise.'

Harry piped in, 'You girls both look great, and Alf and I are pleased to be back. When are we going to meet up and have a snogging session and a few laughs?'

Moira jumped in with, 'Well you know what happened at the last church dance, when Mr Ellison said that because of the fighting it was probably the last one we would have there? Well the vicar knows now that it was not our fault, and apparently we can have another dance at the end of the month, providing Mr Ellison carries out an initial door check as to who comes in, and he's agreed to do it.'

'Oh that's brilliant,' I said.

Looking at Moira, I leaned over, winked and whispered, 'You and I can finish off where we left off the last time, don't you think?'

Returning the wink, Moira whispered back, 'There's a problem with that.'

'What sort of problem?'

'The dance is not until the end of the month.'

Then it clicked, she wanted for us to get together sooner rather than later.

Lynda took hold of Harry's arm, saying, 'Now let's hear all about this exciting holiday, and don't leave anything out.'

'So much has happened,' replied Harry. 'We may not be able to remember everything that we have done. Are your parents in or out today?'

'They are out; they've gone to see my uncle and they won't be back till late. So you and Alf can come over for a cup of tea, it may help you to remember.'

'A stiff drink might help.'

As we walked off, I put my arm around Moira's shoulder, saying, 'As Harry said, we've done an awful lot during the holiday, I will have to bring you up to speed.'

'Can Lynda and I come on holiday with you next time?'

'I'm not sure about that, you see the problem is, Eddie from the dairy asked us before we left to go on holiday, if he and his mate could come with us on the next one.'